SUBLUNARY

Other books by R. A. Steffan

The Last Vampire: Books 1-3
The Last Vampire: Books 4-6

Vampire Bound: Book One
Vampire Bound: Book Two
Vampire Bound: Book Three
Vampire Bound: Book Four

Forsaken Fae: Book One
Forsaken Fae: Book Two
Forsaken Fae: Book Three

The Sixth Demon: Book One
The Sixth Demon: Book Two
The Sixth Demon: Book Three
The Sixth Demon: Book Four

Circle of Blood: Books 1-3
Circle of Blood: Books 4-6

The Complete Horse Mistress Collection
The Complete Lion Mistress Collection
The Complete Dragon Mistress Collection
The Complete Master of Hounds Collection

Antidote: Love and War, Book 1
Antigen: Love and War, Book 2
Antibody: Love and War, Book 3
Anthelion: Love and War, Book 4
Antagonist: Love and War, Book 5

Liminal: The Morpheus Trilogy, Book One

SUBLUNARY

R. A. STEFFAN

TABLE OF CONTENTS

ONE

HUGH GAZED OUT across a field of brilliant red, dotted here and there with lighter blotches of purple and lavender. "Are those…?" he began.

"Poppies?" His companion raised a raven-dark eyebrow. "Yes. For many, the Night Lands are a place of forgetting. Or, at least, a place of setting down one's burdens for a time."

Morpheus seemed somehow *more himself* in this strange dreamscape of gently waving flowers and golden half-light. It was hard to describe — he looked the same as he did in the waking world, but there was a certain tension, a certain fish-out-of-water aura surrounding him there that appeared absent here.

Hugh tore his attention away from the perfectly sculpted profile with difficulty, in favor of turning a slow circle. Taking everything in. "It's not nearly as… uh… *dark* as I expected from the name."

Morpheus exhaled a small huff of amusement. "Perhaps not this part of it. You might feel differently, were you to visit my uncle in Tartarus. Which, by the way, I would not recommend."

In recent centuries, Hugh had possessed more reason than most to keep up with his classical mythology, so it didn't take long to dredge the name from his memory.

"The pit where deceased souls are judged for eternal punishment? Yeah, thanks—I'm good." He paused, letting the words sink in for a moment. "So, all that stuff is real, then. *Terrific.* Really, that's just wonderful."

Morpheus turned his head just enough to give Hugh the side-eye. "I feel compelled to point out that you were the one who decided to kick the God of Death in the groin six hundred years ago."

"He was annoying me," Hugh retorted, feeling his ears heat. "So were you, for that matter. You were just smart enough to stay out of striking range."

The faintest curl of amusement graced Morpheus' full lips.

Hugh tried not to stare at that lush mouth.

Failed abysmally.

Sighed.

After a few helplessly moonstruck moments, he cleared his throat. "I imagine you're glad to be back. Have you let your family know you're here?"

As soon as the words left his lips, he realized how potentially fraught they were. This was confirmed when an implacable mask slipped over Morpheus' expression, erasing the traces of amusement as though they'd never been.

"Not yet," his companion murmured.

Before Hugh could stumble over some kind of apology for bringing up a subject as complicated as Morpheus' family, movement in the air above them caught his eye.

"Iridaceae!" he exclaimed, as the owl glided neatly down to land on Morpheus' outstretched arm, flapping a couple of times to gain balance. "Your wing is better!"

Iridaceae preened, stretching the wing out to show off the glossy feathers.

"She is healed," Morpheus said simply. "As I told you, it was only a matter of getting her here, where my powers are strong enough to fix the damage."

Something about his tone made Hugh examine him more closely. "And what about you? Did coming here heal you as well?"

A look of vexation furrowed Morpheus' brow, as though he were unaccustomed to people asking after his welfare. He drew breath—but before he could speak, Iridaceae hopped down from her perch on his arm, transforming even as her feet touched the ground.

"Why do you think he hasn't talked to his family yet?" she asked dryly.

"Clothing, Iridaceae," Morpheus prompted.

Iridaceae made a disgruntled noise, and a light, toga-like dress materialized, draping over her slender body from shoulder to knee.

"It's really good to see you, sweetheart," Hugh said with sincere relief. "You're okay now?"

She shrugged a shoulder carelessly, the arm attached to it now straight and unblemished rather than twisted and broken. "Why wouldn't I be?" Her tawny eyes narrowed, darting between them. "Wait. Have you two been doing naked stuff again?"

Her accusing gaze landed on her master.

Hugh sighed, resigned to the weirdness that his dreaming life had apparently become. "Maybe a little bit. Don't knock it 'til you've tried it, yeah?"

"Such things are not a suitable topic for conversation, Iridaceae," Morpheus told her firmly.

She snorted. "Try telling that to Phantasos. Do you have any idea how much time I had to spend sucking up to that conceited prat while you were gone? Because *it was a lot.*"

"And I, for one, appreciate your sacrifice," Hugh said, before Morpheus could get a word in. "If you hadn't found a way to reach me on Earth and let me know what was happening, our mutual friend might still be stuck in that bunker."

Iridaceae beamed under the praise, and Morpheus softened visibly.

"He is correct. Your loyalty and resourcefulness have been noted, Iridaceae," Morpheus said. "However, any discussion of my private matters—and Hugh's—remains inappropriate. Did you have anything else to report to me?"

"No," Iridaceae replied, not seeming much concerned by the rebuke. "Mostly, I just wanted to see Hugh."

She bounced forward and wrapped her arms around Hugh's neck, taking him by surprise. He hugged her back tightly.

"Thanks for getting him back," she whispered in his ear before stepping away. "Oh, and tell Baphometh I said hello."

With that, she transformed once more, flapping away on silent wings.

Hugh blinked after her. "Right. Tell my cat that the shapeshifting owl girl says hi. I'll make a note." He hesitated. "Or possibly not. Am I going to remember all of this when I wake up?"

"Yes," Morpheus said. "You will."

A sense of relief washed over him. "Oh, good. There are several parts of the last few hours that I'd hate to lose."

Morpheus wandered slowly through the sea of poppies, his hand trailing among the blooms. Hugh paced him, more interested in the play of subtle emotion across his face than their fantastical surroundings.

When the God of Dreams finally spoke, it was with an unaccustomed hesitance. "I am unsure whether I have adequately conveyed the risk you take by accepting a place at my side. It would perhaps be for the best were you not to draw attention to yourself, or to our... *arrangement.*"

"Morpheus," Hugh said, "I honestly have no idea what our *arrangement* even entails. Not in practical terms. But whatever it is, I'm pretty sure it won't be improved by pretending it doesn't exist."

Morpheus continued walking; his blue eyes focused straight ahead. He was silent for long enough that the atmosphere between them grew heavy. Still, Hugh refused to break it.

"You asked if I was recovered fully from my ordeal," Morpheus said eventually. "The answer is no — I am not. You are placing yourself in a vulnerable position at a time when I am ill-equipped to protect you from harm."

Exasperation for this impossible creature walking next to him swelled in Hugh's chest. He reached out, hooking Morpheus by one arm and pulling him to a stop. They faced each other among the sea of flowers, Morpheus frowning down at Hugh from his slight advantage of height.

Hugh resisted the urge to shake him. "*Morpheus*. The point here is that I *want to help you*. Which I can't do if I'm busy pretending we've never met, and that I don't give a shit about you. So, here's what's going to happen. When I wake up, I'm going to track down Philomena *fucking* Waldenpole and figure out if she's after you for her own purposes, or if someone else put her up to it. And by someone else, I mean your creepy brother."

Morpheus drew himself up straight, his expression vexed. "You must not attempt to confront Phobetor."

"Because that admonition worked *so well* in the eighteenth century," Hugh said, deadpan.

"You do not understand what you are dealing with when it comes to the divine," Morpheus shot back, his expression darkening.

"Maybe I don't," Hugh said, "but that's not going to stop me. In case you've forgotten, the divine dropped itself in my lap eight hundred years ago; I didn't go seeking it out."

He still had his grip on Morpheus' arm, and he used it now to reel him in until their foreheads rested against each other, mildly astonished when Morpheus allowed the manhandling.

"My point is," Hugh told him, "you're not alone."

In the next moment, Hugh's surroundings swirled into a gray blur, vertigo assailing him. He awoke on the ratty green sofa in his sitting room, to the soft tap of Baphometh's paw on his cheek, demanding breakfast.

"*Bollocks*," he said groggily, shooing the animal away and sitting up.

Somehow, he felt the last part of that conversation—assuming it had truly been real—could have gone a lot better.

TWO

AFTER THROWING HIS ruined pajama bottoms in the laundry and checking the sofa cushions for any unfortunate semen stains, Hugh fed his bloody nuisance of a tomcat.

"Iridaceae says hello," he told the troublesome little creature. "And I can't believe I'm actually passing on a dream message to a cat."

"*Mrow*," replied the cat.

"I'll tell her you said so, assuming I see her again," he promised.

Hugh ate a couple of pieces of toast with marmalade for his own breakfast and then went to take a shower, trying very hard not to picture alabaster skin gleaming with rivulets of warm water. Morpheus hadn't been lying when he'd assured Hugh that he would remember his dream. However, Hugh wasn't currently certain whether that was a blessing or a curse.

Great sex or not, the way they'd left things was… less than ideal.

There was no way Hugh would leave the loose thread that was Philomena Waldenpole dangling in the breeze, waiting to unravel catastrophically at some random future date. He was more than a little cross with himself for having been so completely taken in. Had Philomena been playing him from the start? Or had she simply seen an opportunity to grab power for herself and taken it?

Either way, she was very much responsible for the death of a troubled young woman. And, briefly, for *Hugh's* death—not that dying ever seemed to slow him down in the grand scheme of things. Then there was Iridaceae's injury, not to mention the additional suffering she'd indirectly caused Morpheus by forcing him to witness both of those things.

All in all, Hugh wasn't best pleased with Philomena, and he intended to make sure she knew it.

First, he just had to track her down. Preferably, while not also obsessing about what the hell it meant to be the *'concubinus'* of a minor deity who inhabited the world of sleep and dreams. Christ… Hugh really was thoroughly fucked, wasn't he? And not just in the fun way.

What did he think he was going to do if it turned out Phobetor was somehow behind Philomena's actions? He let out a wry snort. Based on historical precedent, chances were he'd end up having a panic attack and fainting on the spot.

Still, at least they'd know. Hugh didn't necessarily have to confront Morpheus' terrifying brother directly. He just needed intel. He remembered from his first run-in with the God of Fear that there were rules about deities interfering in the mortal realm. That implied there were also some sort of arbiters of godly behavior. Maybe he and Morpheus didn't need to deal with this themselves, assuming they could gather proof and submit it to whoever enforced the laws in the Night Lands.

And… now he was thinking about the Night Lands again.

Assuming this nebulous romantic relationship didn't explode spectacularly in Hugh's face, did Morpheus intend to conduct their affair exclusively in the dream world? In reality, he had no idea if his history of centenary meetings with the Nightmare God constituted the extent of Morpheus' forays into the human realm, or whether he popped in for tea on a regular basis and just couldn't be bothered to visit Hugh more often than once a century.

Hugh shook his head sharply, making a concerted attempt to derail that unproductive line of thought before it took hold. He dressed. He checked his schedule to make sure there weren't any more farrier appointments that needed cancelling. He pondered the wisdom of turning all his regular clients over to Steph, the hungry young blacksmith who was making inroads in the next county over.

Deciding it was too early for that kind of drastic action, he turned his attention back to the problem of Philomena. She wasn't answering her phone — not a huge surprise. He sent her a neutral-sounding email, which wasn't as easy to pull off as it sounded, given the circumstances. Honestly, he didn't expect a response to that, either.

Her website was still up, but it was just a set of static pages. There was no way to glean where she was. No blog or recent social media updates. Next, he went looking for information on a bloke named Terry with ties to the paranormal artifact market. That took ages, and when he finally found a likely candidate, there was no way to know for certain whether it was the same man who'd notified Philomena about Dierdre and the mysterious key.

Banking on the unlikelihood of there being more than one Terry operating in such a niche area, Hugh left messages for him as well. By that time, it was coming up on two o'clock in the afternoon. He ate more toast, made a mental note to buy food, and debated with himself for fifteen minutes about the wisdom of driving to Philomena's house in London.

In the end, he did so—simply because that seemed like the most straightforward way to find her if she hadn't scarpered already.

Traffic was dreadful on the trip up, but he reached the neat, semi-detached brick house a couple of hours later. No one answered the door, and when he peeked through the mail slot, it was to find more than a single day's worth of mail lying on the floor.

"Can I help you, young man?" came a sharp voice from the street.

Hugh looked up from his obvious snooping to find an elderly man watching him suspiciously. A neighbor, he assumed.

"Yes, sorry," he said. "I'm an old friend of Philomena's. We were supposed to get together for lunch, but she hasn't been responding to phone messages or email for the past few days. I'm a bit worried about her, to be honest. Have you seen her recently?"

The old man's expression didn't soften. "Can't say as I have. Maybe you'd do better to call the police if you're worried, rather than peering through her letterbox."

"Sorry," Hugh said again. "You're right, of course. I'll let them know. See if maybe they'll send someone out to do a welfare check."

The man gave a sharp nod, and continued to watch him like a hawk until he got back in his van and drove away.

Defeated for today, Hugh returned to Long Sutton by way of the nearest ASDA, where he at least succeeded in picking up some groceries. Neither Terry the artifact enthusiast nor Philomena herself had left him any messages. For the moment, that left him at something of a dead end. He went for a walk in the woods as the sun was sinking below the horizon to clear his head, then rattled around in the house for another couple of hours before retiring to the sofa to sleep.

Given the intermittent nature of his relationship with Morpheus across the centuries, he didn't really expect to experience anything beyond a normal night's rest when he finally dropped off. Even so, his thoughts turned to images of a piercing blue gaze and flawless skin as his eyes slipped closed, memories of hands roaming flesh and rising pleasure following him down into darkness.

❖

Hugh's next awareness was of warm stone beneath his back and cool water washing over his legs. The combination of sensations felt oddly soothing. The smooth stone beneath him molded to his reclining body in a way that seemed... unlikely, somehow? As though a master sculptor had taken a cast of his back and arse and carved the weathered rock to cradle him perfectly.

14

The water receded. He blinked his eyes open groggily staring up at an overcast sky, visible above dramatic cliffs. A fresh wave crashed over his lower body with more force, peppering him with sea spray. Startled, he tried to jerk upright into a sitting position, only to come up against matching sharp tugs on his wrists.

Hugh rolled his head, first to one side, then the other, glaring when his gaze landed on heavy iron shackles bolted directly into the living stone. He yanked at the restraints fruitlessly. There was no give to them at all… unlike the long, delicate golden chains that had bound him symbolically to Morpheus' bed the last time they'd—

Realization penetrated at the same moment a gentler wave lapped up to his waist, retreating only to his ankles this time when it washed back toward the sea.

"Oh," he told the uncaring sky. "I'm dreaming again." After another searching look at his surroundings, he muttered, "What the *fuck*, brain?"

The shackles we choose for ourselves…

It was nothing more than the memory of a voice. The ghost of words. Even so, Hugh shivered.

The air was warm, although the sun that had heated his cradle of stone had disappeared behind gray clouds. The water washed up to his chest, receding to his knees. *Tide's coming in*, he thought, without the surge of instinctive panic that should have been associated with such a thing.

Again, his background in classical mythology tossed up a relevant reference. *Andromeda chained to the rocks as a sacrifice for the sea monster*. There had been a rather extraordinary statue done by a bloke in America, he recalled — the same one who'd done the Lincoln Memorial statue. Hugh remembered being quite taken with the erotic overtones of the marble representation — a nude beauty reclining on the rocks, helplessly chained by the wrist.

Apparently, he'd been a little *too* taken with it.

Still, it all added up to imply that a handsome rescuer would be appearing momentarily to free him, presumably before he ended up becoming sea monster kibble. So, that was all right. The water washed over his stomach, retreating only as far as his thighs this time. He lay back, wondering vaguely if Morpheus would ride in on a flying horse, or if he'd opt for the original interpretation of the story and fly in on winged sandals instead.

Something brushed his left foot, and he yelped in surprise, craning his head up to stare at the dark, roiling water. The… *whatever* it was… curled around his ankle, spiraling up his calf like a boa constrictor.

"Right," Hugh gasped, jerking against the sinuous hold without effect. "Sea monster. *Fuck.*"

A second tentacle wrapped around his other leg, pinning him in place, spreadeagled. The first continued its upward trajectory as the next wave sloshed over Hugh's chest. He jerked, his heart rabbiting with a heady combination of fear and perverse excitement as the tip slid between his balls and the crease of his inner thigh.

His vision swam for a moment as thoughts of what kind of damage that tentacle could do swirled together with the increasingly desperate mantra — *it's just a dream, it's just a dream.*

The slender appendage curled around the base of his testicles, firmly enough to thwart their new mission of retracting fully into his abdomen, never to be seen again. The tip of the tentacle slid delicately along the length of his cock, which gave a contrary twitch of interest that had nothing to do with either sanity or the concept of self-preservation.

Hugh made another desperately undignified noise as the water receded, baring the sleek, black appendage to his view. It was shiny — smooth on top and with small, regularly spaced suckers running down the bottom in two parallel rows.

The next wave washed in, obscuring the disturbing sight once more. Instead, something large and pale rose from the depths between Hugh's forcibly outstretched legs. A familiar dark-haired head breeched the surface, followed by slender shoulders, a defined chest and stomach, and a strange ombre transition to the same dark, shiny hide that covered the tentacles, beginning where the figure's hips should be.

Morpheus braced himself above Hugh's torso on both arms, a small furrow marring his brow as he scanned their surroundings.

"Interesting choice of venue tonight," he said blandly, returning his attention to his captive sacrifice.

Hugh gaped up at him, wordless.

THREE

"NO OFFENSE," Hugh managed, staring at the odd transitional zone between human torso and tentacle monster, "but that looks… anatomically unlikely?"

Morpheus spared a glance down at his transformed body and raised an eyebrow. "Perhaps so. But, once again, this is *your* dream. Berating me about the details seems rather unproductive."

"Fair." Hugh made a concerted — and largely unsuccessful — attempt to ignore the way one of the clever, prehensile appendages continued to twine around his balls.

Morpheus tilted his head curiously. "Perhaps I should take comfort in the knowledge that your subconscious, at least, understands the danger I represent to you." The tentacle gave an experimental tug on Hugh's scrotum.

Hugh gasped, not proud of the way his dick surged to full hardness in response. Nor was he proud of the way his voice went up half an octave. "Are we really going to have this conversation *now*, Morpheus? For Christ's —"

The words cut off abruptly, replaced by a needy whine as a new tentacle wormed its way down between his arse cheeks and pressed inside his hole, the slender tip slick with slime as it burrowed deeper.

"As long as you appreciate that the appetites of a god will inevitably devour a human," Morpheus said. His eyes grew half-lidded with pleasure as he eased his way into Hugh's body with languid, wriggling thrusts. "Even an immortal one."

A wave washed up to Hugh's collarbones before retreating. "Is that what we're calling this?" Heat radiated outward from the place where they were joined, suckers dragging against Hugh's rim as the tentacle stretched him wider. "Because 'devouring' —*ah!*— isn't the first word that comes to mind."

Morpheus made a considering noise. The other tentacle moved to wrap snugly around the base of Hugh's cock as well as his balls. It gave another firm squeeze, and Hugh arched, jerking against the manacles.

"Perhaps you should consider me the tide, rather than the monster," Morpheus said. A third tentacle rolled out of the water and draped over Hugh's throat, heavier and thicker than the others. "That metaphor seems considerably more apt, under the circumstances. Now, however, I believe we have already discussed your verbosity when I'm attempting to fuck you."

Hugh pushed against the pressure on his neck, lifting his head far enough to glare up at Morpheus. "You conceited—*mmph!*"

The tip of the new appendage took advantage of his open mouth to plunge past Hugh's lips, effectively gagging him. It was blunter and differently shaped than the ones tormenting his arse and cock— a generous mouthful, to put it mildly.

"Mmm," Morpheus purred. "Yes. That's much better."

Hugh made a noise of outrage that did nothing to hide how hard his dick twitched as Morpheus began to fuck his face with leisurely intent, head thrown back in sensual gratification.

To say Hugh was out of practice with deep-throating was a serious understatement. For better or worse, Morpheus was the one doing all the work, though—and before long, a thick spurt of liquid exploded over Hugh's tongue—briny with a hint of sweetness lurking beneath. Hugh swallowed convulsively, trying not to choke. Within moments, a pleasant feeling of warmth bloomed in his esophagus, spreading downward to his stomach and, a few seconds later, upward to his brain.

The muscles of his throat relaxed. Every nerve felt like it was firing in double-time, oversensitive and pleasure-drunk. The two tentacles breaching him pressed deeper in tandem, their way easing. A fresh burst of liquid dribbled down his gullet, and this time the noise he made was less protesting and more pleading.

The strange hypersensitivity rolled outward through his body until it encompassed every part of him. Each slow thrust from the magnificent creature ravishing him felt like it would tip him into a full-body orgasm, only the stranglehold Morpheus kept on his balls and the base of his dick preventing Hugh from blowing his load in seconds.

The water, which had been creeping inexorably higher throughout all of this, washed over his chin and along his cheeks. Some remaining shred of instinct had him craning up, trying to get his face clear. The tentacle draped over his throat urged him down again until he once more lay supine on the oddly comfortable rock.

The pressure against his windpipe was inexorable, yet it somehow felt tender at the same time. By contrast, the punishing double thrust into his mouth and arse was blissfully brutal… as though the two tentacles might eventually meet in the middle if they kept going long enough, shaking hands somewhere in the vicinity of his stomach.

Again, orgasm threatened, held at bay only by the implacable living cock ring that prevented his balls from drawing up in readiness to spend.

Twice more, the tide-driven waves swelled over them, tickling Hugh's temples and the sides of his nose before sliding away. He shifted restlessly, pinned in place and unable to evade the growing threat, watching Morpheus' expression with a sort of drunken, obsessive fascination. His lover's face had transformed into a feral sort of ecstasy—an entirely different demeanor than that of the martyred angel Hugh had pleasured for hours in the waking world.

Another spurt of salty sweetness rolled down Hugh's throat. Morpheus flung his head back, baring teeth that were too long and too sharp—a predator's teeth, made for tearing out throats.

For devouring, Hugh acknowledged—if only to himself.

Although it was inevitable and should not, therefore, have come as a surprise, the heave and surge of water rushing over Hugh's head and submerging him fully shocked him partway out of his drugged reverie. His strangled noise of protest echoed in his own ears before trailing away in a plume of bubbles. After a few endless seconds, the sea receded, and he spluttered around the tentacle still mercilessly fucking his throat.

The next wave didn't quite manage to swamp him, but the one after that did… along with the next, and the next, and the next. He struggled to breathe in between the swells, drowning as much in the tentacles' endless ejaculate pumping into his mouth and arse as the seawater. Each time, the ruthless dunking lasted longer. Each time, the chance to gasp a lungful of air before he was submerged again grew shorter.

The tentacle reaming his arse shifted its angle, suckers rubbing across his prostate with every rough thrust. Hugh grunted and arched, dragging in a choked half-breath as the sea pulled back and rushed in again with a terrible sort of finality, cutting him off from the world of light and oxygen.

He held onto the precious air with single-minded determination, his eyes open wide, staring at the pale blur of Morpheus poised over him through the cloudy, stinging darkness. Without warning, two new tentacles latched onto his nipples with hungry, sharp-toothed mouths, driving a burst of bubbles from his nose as they bit and sucked at the pebbled peaks.

The same sweet venom that had rendered his mind pliant and his body oversensitive pumped into the swollen nubs, until the rhythmic suction coupled with the needlelike pain of pierced flesh combined into a sweet, unbearable fire. Hugh twisted and thrashed uselessly — trying to get away, trying to get more, feeling the weight of far too much water pressing down on him from above.

His lungs burned, demanding relief that wouldn't come in time. Sparks exploded along his nerves as Morpheus, unburdened by the need to breathe, continued to plow his prostate with cruel precision. Abruptly, the punishing grip around the base of Hugh's balls loosened, the tentacle shifting to spiral firmly around his cock instead. Desperation overtook him, and Hugh thrust into those slick, grasping coils like a madman, his thundering heart pounding a frantic bass drumbeat in his ears.

Once, twice, three times, four times — and all of Hugh's remaining air exploded from his lungs at the same instant his release exploded from his balls, burning its way out of his dick to spurt white clouds of seed into the uncaring sea.

Writhing like a hooked fish, he finally lost the battle with his lungs and dragged in a massive gulp of salt water —

———◆———

— only to jerk upright on his ratty couch with a gasp, spine arching into a bow, stomach muscles jerking as he came like a runaway freight train.

He couldn't *stop*; his balls pumping more and more jizz until it felt like they were trying to turn themselves inside out. His vision wavered, his body shuddering itself into exhaustion before going abruptly and uncompromisingly limp. Falling back against the abused cushions, Hugh stared slack-jawed at the ceiling, barely visible in the weak, early morning light.

"Guess I might as well start sleeping in the bed again," he rasped, past a throat that felt like he'd been screaming for hours. "Clearly, using the couch isn't helping matters."

There was no answer—not even a disdainful meow from Baphometh. Possibly he'd scared the poor beast away into the woods with whatever performance he'd been putting on in his sleep. He was uncomfortably aware of the sticky mess inside his pajama bottoms... and utterly unable to get up and do anything about it, since he couldn't currently feel his legs.

Or his arms.

Or his face.

"I need therapy," he muttered. "Lots and lots of very expensive, very in-depth therapy. *Good Christ.* What the hell is wrong with me?"

Again, nobody answered.

By the time Hugh got all his limbs working, the sun was up and shining merrily through the curtains. Baphometh, who would normally have been begging for food by now, had apparently decided to leave for good and find an owner who wasn't a degenerate pervert. Hugh couldn't really blame him.

He cleaned up—*again*. He ate toast and jam—*again*. He resolutely didn't panic over where on the sexual spectrum one went after having near-fatal underwater tentacle sex with your eldritch horror of a boyfriend on the second date. Or had that been the third date?

Whatever. He *wasn't thinking about that.*

Instead, he was thinking about checking his messages. Because that was his current project—not digging further into the *Kama Sutra: Cult of Cthulhu Edition*. His overworked dick gave a half-hearted twitch of curiosity, and he growled at it in irritation.

Messages, damn it.

There was nothing on his phone. The laptop hummed to life at the press of a button, and Hugh ruthlessly tore through the dozens of spam emails that had started appearing in his inbox within forty-eight hours of opening the bloody account. He flagged them with extreme prejudice and consigned them to the bottomless pit of the trash can icon, until he came to one from *t.culpepper@fantasticarti-facts.co.uk*.

"Now we're getting somewhere," he said to the empty room.

Mr. de Ferrers —

Thank you for reaching out, and for your concern over Ms. Waldenpole's wellbeing. As it happens, I believe she has been traveling these last few days. She contacted me regarding a new artifact only yesterday, and I will be meeting with her at my office this evening to appraise it. I informed her of your message. She immediately invited you to join us there at 7pm if you are so inclined, as the item may be of personal interest to you.

Yours,

Terry Culpepper, Esq.

Owner, Fantastic Artifacts

Paranormal Curios for the Discerning Collector

An address near Tooting Bec followed. Hugh reread the short missive twice, turning it over in his mind. He could make a reasonable guess as to the artifact in question. After the confrontation in the bunker, he'd run off with an injured Morpheus and

Iridaceae in tow, leaving behind a set of chains and shackles powerful enough to bind a god for eighty years in his haste to get away to safety.

If the British government neglected to check on its abandoned WWII bunker on a regular basis, there was no reason someone couldn't have snuck back in and chiseled them free of the concrete floor.

Alternately, it could be something completely unrelated. Hugh doubted it, though. He was also cognizant of the chance that this whole thing might be some sort of bizarre trap. However, an internet search showed that the curio shop was legit... assuming 'legit' was the correct word for a place that mostly sold crystal balls and haunted knick-knacks that weren't actually haunted.

It was a public place located in a bustling city — and while Philomena might be an evil bitch, she was also a frail old woman. Making his decision, Hugh typed out a bland affirmative reply and received confirmation from *Terry Culpepper, Esq.* a few minutes later.

Baphometh reappeared as Hugh was closing down the computer, having apparently decided that free kitty kibble outweighed whatever disturbing behavior he might have witnessed the previous night. Hugh fed him without comment.

He spent the rest of the morning cooking and freezing simple meals for himself using the groceries he'd bought on the way back from London. The afternoon, he devoted to finding out whether Steph, the rival farrier from the next county over, had any interest in picking up most of his current clients. Not surprisingly, she was dead keen on the idea, and thanked him profusely for thinking of her.

With his plate as clear as it could be for the foreseeable future, Hugh climbed into his rattling van and headed for his evening appointment in Tooting Bec.

According to his phone map, *Fantastic Artifacts* was accessed by an unprepossessing door in an alley off Upper Tooting Road. He parked nearby and kept a close watch on his surroundings as he approached the place. There was nothing unusual to be found among the evening bustle of shoppers.

The door was locked, but a handwritten sign had been taped to the glass. 'Ring for service,' it said, with an arrow pointing helpfully toward the bell.

Hugh rang. Less than a minute later, the lock clicked. The door swung open, revealing a stoop-shouldered man in his forties with a long face and a sallow complexion.

"Hello. I'm Hugh de Ferrers," Hugh greeted, holding out a hand. "You must be Mr. Culpepper, I assume?"

"That's right." Terry Culpepper took Hugh's hand in a limp, sweaty grip and gave it a desultory shake. "Do come in, we're just about to get started."

Hugh forced a pleasant smile onto his face and stepped through the door. He only realized his mistake when a sudden movement in his peripheral vision caught his attention. Before he could dodge out of the way, something heavy and solid crashed down on the back of his skull, turning the world black.

FOUR

HUGH REGAINED consciousness to find himself slumped in a heavy wooden chair. Two large men loomed over him, efficiently binding his arms to the armrests. He jerked, discovering in the process that they'd already bound his ankles to the chair's legs.

"Wh-where…?" he began, only for one of the blokes to smack him across the mouth like an abusive parent backhanding a troublesome child. The impact nicked the inside of Hugh's lip against an eye-tooth, and he tasted blood.

Maybe the half-hearted blow jarred something loose in his brain, because recent events started to come back to him. *Philomena. The email from Terry Culpepper. Traveling to the man's shop in… Tooting Bec?*

Yes, that was it. He was in London, presumably in the back room of the optimistically named *Fantastic Artifacts*.

Tied to a chair.

Oops.

He hoped Philomena's associates weren't in the habit of offing people and dumping their bodies in the river. That would be a dismal way to wake up after dying.

The goon who'd smacked him gave the rope around his left wrist a final tug. Then both of the men straightened and stepped back, seemingly satisfied with their work. Without the solid wall of muscle hemming him in from either side, Hugh got a proper view of the room for the first time. It was decently lit, piled high with dusty boxes, and it sported a messy desk with an office chair in one corner—both of which had seen better days.

Terry Culpepper, Esquire stood next to the desk, wringing his hands nervously as he oversaw the restraint of his captive. He didn't really look like the sort of man who hired thugs to hit visitors over the head and tie them up. In fact, he looked terrified.

"Mate," Hugh said, "I don't know what kind of nonsense Philomena has been feeding you—but if you let me go, I'll walk out of here and you'll never have to see me again."

The goon backhanded him on the other cheek. Hugh's head snapped sideways, his cervical vertebrae protesting the whiplash with a jolt of pain.

Philomena walked in. She had the same pale, clammy air of fear as Culpepper, and she looked like she'd aged a decade in the days since Hugh had last seen her. Given her age to begin with, the overall effect was alarming.

"Philomena—" Hugh began.

"Shut up," she snapped, all trace of the eccentric, grandmotherly figure vanishing beneath barely controlled desperation. "Dierdre is dead. The demon is gone! What did you do with it? Did you bind it somehow? Take it for yourself?"

Hugh hesitated for a split second, trying to get his brain functioning properly.

"There was no demon," he said. "The bunker was empty except for a bunch of rubble and some old chains bolted to the floor. Maybe Dierdre came back after I left and committed suicide when she found out her grandfather's story was a fairy tale."

"You're lying!" A manic light illuminated Philomena's bloodshot eyes. "Tell me where you're hiding the creature! I *need* it!"

"Ms. Waldenpole..." Culpepper began uneasily.

She waved him off with an angry gesture.

An unpleasant suspicion had begun to coalesce in Hugh's mind. "Why do you *need* a demon, Philomena? And why are you so convinced there was anything in that bunker to begin with? It was a crazy story from start to finish."

"We retrieved the chains," Culpepper said. "They weren't made of any metal found on Earth. The buyer insisted we—"

"Be quiet, you fool," Philomena hissed.

But Hugh latched onto that, his sense of dread deepening. "What buyer? I don't suppose it was a tall, skinny bloke who looked like a great big walking spider, with a voice like the wind through dry branches? Maybe he called himself Timor?"

Philomena snarled and hobbled over to stand in front of him, grabbing his chin in bony fingers that felt more like claws. "You *do* know something. In fact, you know far more than you're letting on. I want that creature, and you *will* tell me where it is!"

She reeked of fear. It was oozing from her pores like sweat, stirring old memories from Hugh's past.

"Oh, shit. He got to you, didn't he?" The fingers on his jaw tightened, and he could feel their faint tremor. "Timor got to you. What does he want?"

"He took the chains," Culpepper blurted. "He paid us for them with gold, but—"

"But he looked you in the eye, and now it's all you can do not to piss yourself in terror whenever you think about him," Hugh finished.

Philomena jerked her hand away from his face with a frustrated growl. "Get the information out of him," she ordered. "I don't care how."

With that, she whirled and limped out of the room on arthritic joints. Culpepper shot Hugh a fraught look, his eyes darting between the empty doorway and the two goons. One of the thugs cracked his knuckles, rolling his head from side to side to stretch out his neck muscles.

Hugh sighed in resignation. "Go on, then. Don't stick around on my account, Culpepper."

As though Hugh's permission had freed him from his paralysis, the shopkeeper bolted from the room as though the hounds of hell were after him. Hugh supposed, in a way, that they were.

—————◆—————

The next few hours were unpleasant in a way Hugh hadn't experienced in quite some time. When the hired thugs eventually got tired of listening to Hugh's ridiculous and contradictory answers in between rounds of beatings, they conferred briefly and left the room, locking the door behind them with a decisive *snick*.

They might've gone out for a fag, or a piss, or a bite to eat. Or they might be planning to leave Hugh here, bruised, battered, and tied to a chair, until exhaustion and thirst loosened his tongue.

As minutes ticked by into hours, it became apparent that it was the latter. Hugh closed his eyes and let his head slump forward, having had more practice than most people at resting while held in uncomfortable and inhumane conditions.

His spine might never forgive him, but eventually, the elusive fingers of sleep stroked through his hair, settling deeper and stealing his mind away from the waking world.

Hugh blinked his eyes open to the sight of rustling leaves waving overhead in a gentle breeze, late afternoon sunlight filtering through the ever-moving branches to dapple the ground with ruddy gold.

"I know this place," said a bemused voice—rich, familiar velvet layered over cool marble. "Your mind only brings you here when you are particularly troubled."

Hugh's head was resting on a hard-muscled thigh. The fingers running over his scalp felt inhumanly smooth. Morpheus was sprawled indolently against the trunk of the massive oak where Hugh and Agnes used to come to escape the midafternoon heat of summer, in the clearing south of their cottage.

"Hi," he said stupidly, his brain mired in the illogic of sleep. "No tentacles this time?" He tilted his head back until he was looking up at the hawklike features poised above him.

Morpheus canted an eyebrow. "It's *your*—"

"My dream. Yes, I know," Hugh finished for him. "Still, I feel like I should send you my dry-cleaning bill." He swallowed a sigh. "I don't suppose you could drop by the waking world—the

32

Sublunary, I think you called it—for a visit one of these days? I miss seeing you in my bed."

Clearly, the lack of a brain-to-mouth filter that seemed to plague him in dreams was back in full force.

The eyebrow lowered. "I fear not." Morpheus hesitated, as though debating whether to continue. "I am still too weak to travel between the realms at will. Returning to the Night Lands consumed much of the power you gifted me, and my attempt to undo the damage of neglect caused by my absence has so far precluded regaining my strength. At least beyond the minimum needed to function in my duties."

Hugh closed his eyes and nodded, resigned. "Are people dreaming normally now? Everyone, I mean—not just me?"

Again, Morpheus hesitated. "The injury to the collective unconscious of sentient beings was not inconsiderable. I am... doing the best I can, in the absence of so many of my oneiri."

Hugh reached up and grasped the hand that had stilled in its stroking of his hair, tangling their fingers together. He brought it to his lips, kissing the smooth knuckles.

"You're only one person, *leof*," he murmured, the Middle English endearment slipping from his lips unbidden.

"I am a god," Morpheus corrected.

"Fine," Hugh said. "You're only one *god*, then." The words jarred something in his memory. He sat up abruptly, dropping Morpheus' hand. "Oh, *hell*. I've just remembered. Your brother. The terrifying one, not the smarmy one. He's up to something on Earth."

Morpheus froze, his features hardening. "You have ignored my instructions to leave Phobetor and his scheming well alone?"

Hugh frowned. "Don't get your knickers in a twist, love. I tracked down Philomena Waldenpole, just like I told you I was going to do. Turns out she went back to the bunker and retrieved those chains that were holding you. Phobetor must've found out somehow, because he showed up to buy them off her and her accomplice. He did a number on her — or rather, on both of them. They're acting like terrified wrecks. And Philomena's absolutely *desperate* to find you, which I'm guessing means Phobetor wants to get to you."

Morpheus' expression resembled a thundercloud. "And this *Philomena* told you all these things?"

Hugh coughed and rubbed the back of his neck sheepishly. "Er… yes. About that. I might've… accidentally let myself get captured?"

The clearing grew darker, as though storm clouds were rolling in, or the moon was sliding across the sun, eclipsing it.

"Anyway, most of it came out while Philomena and her two hired goons were trying to get me to tell them how to find you," he finished.

"You have been captured?" The velvet voice turned dangerous.

Hugh shrugged, unable to deny it.

"You will accompany me to my palace," Morpheus said, in the tone of an order. "I would have you identify this *Philomena* for me, that I may enter her dreams and punish her for daring to lay hands on you."

Hugh blinked, because that pronouncement was... kind of a lot, actually.

"Right," he said slowly. "Or... and hear me out on this part... you could let me handle things, because she's an octogenarian who's clearly terrified out of her mind by your brother, and driving her insane with nightmares isn't going to help us learn anything else about Phobetor's plans."

Morpheus drew breath to speak, the sound sharp and irritated. Before he could, pain exploded across Hugh's temple, his head snapping sideways even as his surroundings wavered and dissolved into mist.

The shock propelled him back into consciousness inside a cramped room full of boxes, where two irritated thugs glared down at him with matching stony expressions.

FIVE

MORPHEUS STOOD SLOWLY as the remnants of Hugh's dream faded away like wisps of vapor—leaving him alone in his palace, surrounded by mirrors. Slow rage rolled through his veins. It was difficult to separate the part of it directed at the human called *Philomena Waldenpole* from the part directed at Hugh himself for his foolishness.

Morpheus had *told* him not to pursue this course. Had *ordered* him, for Hugh's own safety. Hugh had ignored that command, and now it appeared he was suffering the consequences.

A tiny voice of rationality pointed out that Hugh was immortal, and he had doubtless endured things far more dangerous than a rough interrogation by other humans. That small voice was immediately drowned out by a cacophony of fresh worry. Phobetor had visited Hugh's captors, apparently not long before the human was captured. The God of Fear might return at any time, and if his brother encountered Hugh there... if he *remembered* him—

Morpheus swept out of the room in a violent swirl of robes.

"*Iridaceae!*" he called, letting the summons echo throughout his domain, spreading through the ether until it thundered.

His familiar came flying through the corridor at speed a few moments later, correctly interpreting the urgency behind his demand for her presence.

She flapped to a landing in front of him, reality twisting as she shifted into her human form. "What is it, what's happened?" she asked, breathless.

"I must travel to the Sublunary immediately," he said, biting off the words. "Something there requires my presence without delay."

Her eyes narrowed. "Hang on. Are you strong enough for that? I thought—"

"I am not," he snapped. "Which is why I require your assistance. Hugh de Ferrers is in danger."

She blinked at him. "Oh." Concern creased her elfin features. A moment later, her expression soured as understanding of what he needed from her penetrated. "*Oh*. Right. Well, *this* is going to suck..."

———◆———

Finding Hugh de Ferrers in the waking world had become almost second nature over the centuries. London was still one of the humans' great metropolises, and Morpheus recognized its aura as he wrenched himself through the veil with far more effort than should have been required.

The room where he reappeared was squalid and dusty. It smelled of stale sweat and blood. Three people occupied the central space. One stood off to the side. The second was tied to a chair. The third loomed over the bound man, a fist drawn back to strike.

The threatened blow landed an instant later with a meaty thump, drawing a wheezing grunt of pain from the man in the chair. Morpheus stepped out of the shadow of a pile of boxes, his lip curled in a snarl. The attacker's head jerked up; his attention caught by the unexpected appearance of a figure in the corner of his eye. His fellow interrogator whirled around as well, following his startled gaze.

"What the hell?" the second man asked, scrabbling inside his shapeless jacket—presumably for a weapon.

The memory of gunshots, of blood, of *pain*, whispered through the back of Morpheus' mind, weaving a thread of unwelcome coldness through the heat of his anger. But this creature was unlikely to have a clip of rune-inscribed bullets ready to fire… and anyway, it was too late. Already, darkness filled the room like a black tide, creeping up the humans' legs—even as they screamed and batted at their clothing, as though trying to brush off swarming insects.

Their deepest nightmares filtered into Morpheus' awareness.

Fire.

Suffocation.

With a sneer, Morpheus crafted their personal torments into an ever-contracting spiral inside their minds, setting them to replay over and over, faster and faster. The screams grew choked. The men crashed to their hands and knees, then scrabbled backward into the chaotic piles of boxes, which tumbled to the floor in a cascade of dusty papers and packing material.

Hugh, still tied to his chair, let out a low moan of pain. Morpheus took a moment to ensure that the darkness hadn't inadvertently touched him. It had not—but from the look of it, serious injury had already been done.

The sound of muffled footsteps from outside the room filtered through the firmly shut door.

"Wh-what's going on in there?" came a male voice, muted by two inches of wood. The words sounded shaky with guilt and fear.

Teeth bared, Morpheus strode over and wrenched the door open, revealing a thin, stoop-shouldered human standing outside. The newcomer wielded a cricket bat with the air of someone who'd never played the sport in his life—much less done physical violence to another person. A wrinkled, elderly woman hovered a few steps behind him, her parchment skin gray with dread.

Morpheus recognized his brother Phobetor's touch upon the two humans standing before him. He recalled Hugh's words.

I tracked down Philomena Waldenpole, just like I told you I was going to do. Turns out she went back to the bunker and retrieved those chains that were holding you. Phobetor must've found out somehow, because he showed up to buy them off her and her accomplice. He did a number on her — or rather, on both of them. They're acting like terrified wrecks.

"Philomena Waldenpole," Morpheus growled, and was rewarded with a startled indrawn breath from the woman.

It was acknowledgement enough.

The cricket bat slid free of the man's nerveless hands, clattering to the floor. He shot his companion a wide-eyed look of panic—even as unnatural darkness rolled past Morpheus, flooding the hallway where the pair stood. Morpheus lifted his chin and let the nightmares come.

Dreams of falling.

Horrific visions of teeth falling out, leaving gaping holes behind.

The man made a terrible noise in his throat and ran, hands scrabbling at his mouth. His shoulder slammed into the wall as he staggered sideways and went down.

The woman—*Philomena*—flailed, her frail limbs jerking. She collapsed to the floor, breath locked in her lungs, trapped in the moment of existential terror just before a fatal impact with jagged rocks.

It would not, Morpheus reflected without emotion, take very long for her heart to give out.

Satisfied, he let the darkness recede, pulling the depths of night back inside himself. Manifesting his powers in the Sublunary had been a drain, as almost everything seemed to be these days. Yet he could not bring himself to regret it as he returned to the beaten captive bound among the piles of fallen boxes.

Hugh, slumped in the chair, looked up at Morpheus through an eye swollen half shut. The other eye was nothing more than a shiny slit surrounded by mottled black and purple.

"What did you do?" he rasped.

In lieu of an answer, Morpheus grabbed the coils of rope binding Hugh's left wrist to the chair and snapped them with effortless strength, repeating the process with the rope around his other wrist and his ankles.

"Morpheus." Hugh's voice sounded like broken glass. He wrapped a newly freed arm around his ribcage as though to support cracked ribs. *"What did you do?"*

One of the interrogators was rocking back and forth, a low, continuous moan issuing from his lips. The other curled in the fetal position, sobbing.

"I punished your captors," Morpheus said simply.

The front of the human's button-down shirt gaped, the undershirt beneath torn open to the navel. Small, circular cigarette burns tracked up and down the length of his torso, leaving patches of his chest hair singed.

Hugh stared at the gibbering men in the corner, half-hidden by fallen boxes.

"Philomena," he croaked. "Did you—"

"She is no longer a concern." Morpheus watched Hugh with a furrowed brow, reaching out a hesitant hand when the human moved to rise.

Predictably, Hugh's legs failed to hold him, and Morpheus grasped him by the biceps to support him. Hugh wavered for a moment before locking his knees and taking his own weight. He batted Morpheus off impatiently and stumbled toward the open door, grasping the wooden frame to support himself.

From that undignified position, he stared down at Philomena Waldenpole. The woman lay twitching on the ground with her unblinking gaze focused on the ceiling. Hugh looked past her, to where the thin man sat crumpled in a heap at the end of the hall. Blood streamed from his mouth as he clawed fitfully at his gums.

"Why?" Hugh breathed.

Morpheus frowned at him, uncomprehending. "They harmed you."

Hugh looked at him with an expression of equal incomprehension shining from his half-open eye.

"This woman was eighty years old if she was a day," he said. "And it's not like they could have killed me." Then something else seemed to occur to him. "Wait. How are you even *here*? I thought you were too weak to travel between realities."

Morpheus felt his lips press into a thin line. "I drained Iridaceae's life force to strengthen myself. It was necessary."

Absolute silence fell between them, broken only by the sounds of humans trapped in nightmare.

"You did *what*?" Hugh demanded. "And no, it bloody well *wasn't* necessary!" He gestured at the crumpled bodies. "How the *hell* do you expect to get any information about Phobetor out of them now?"

"I do not," Morpheus said icily. "And you should not have been attempting to do so. I have been clear on this subject. The matter is not your concern. It is too dangerous for you to pursue Phobetor. I absolutely forbid you from continuing this folly."

Hugh, hunched pathetically in the doorway, gaped at him.

He would heal, Morpheus reminded himself for approximately the dozenth time since arriving in the room. *He would heal.* Somehow, that knowledge did nothing to salve the unpleasant tangle of emotions swirling inside him. Anger. Fear. Frustration. Betrayal.

He had attempted to keep Hugh from pursuing dangerous things—Morpheus himself, foremost among them. And still, the human had defied him at every turn, dismissing his warnings and charging headlong into danger.

This feeling of helplessness was *intolerable*. It was the reason he had always resisted letting others close enough to hurt him with their own pain. He had always considered it safer to remain alone — except for Iridaceae, whom he could at least protect from harm.

Iridaceae never defied him as Hugh had done, stumbling into danger at exactly the time when Morpheus was too weak to help.

"This..." Hugh paused. Swallowed. Licked his split lip, only to wince at the pain. He tried again. "This is a little more fire and brimstone than I thought I was signing up for, your *godship*." The little barb of sarcasm sank home. "I may *only* be human, but I make my own decisions, and no offense — you're being kind of a lot right now."

The coldness that had been threaded around the edges of Morpheus' hot anger spread, chilling him through. Had that not been the point from the beginning? He was a god. He was far too *much* for any creature of the Sublunary to handle. Even an immortal one. It should be a relief that Hugh had finally recognized and accepted this.

It was not a relief.

Somehow, that made the situation even more galling.

He'd hesitated too long before speaking. Hugh, still regarding him with wariness, turned to square up to him in the doorway.

"You said you '*drained*' Iridaceae. I swear to—" Hugh hesitated. "—to *something*, if you've harmed her just so you could come down here and save my sorry arse..."

Morpheus glared at him icily, which only seemed to increase Hugh's alarm.

"Wait," he said, his face going abruptly pale beneath the livid bruises. "She's... she's not... you didn't—"

"*Stop*." Morpheus cut Hugh off before his lover could accuse him—apparently—of murdering his own familiar on a whim. He stepped back, his frustration over the entire situation coalescing into a single, burning point of ice centered within his ribcage. "Clearly, this relationship was a mistake."

Before Hugh could draw breath to reply, Morpheus drew the scraps of his borrowed power around himself and wrenched his form through the veil—returning to his own realm, and the simplicity of his natural state of solitude.

Returning to a place where no infuriating humans attempted to burrow through his defenses, piercing his heart as surely as Professor Rainey's thrice-damned magic-inscribed bullet.

SIX

A WEEK AFTER stumbling out of *Fantastic Artifacts* with a torn shirt, cracked ribs, and a face that looked like he'd gone ten rounds with Joe Calzaghe, Hugh was still boiling mad. It was, he'd decided, a safer reaction than any others that might have presented themselves.

He was uncomfortably aware of how little power he had in this situation. His dreams for the past several days had been, well, *normal*. Whatever that even meant after the decades Morpheus had been held captive. He remembered that he'd dreamt, but he didn't remember many details about the subject of those dreams.

Some of them had been bad, as one might expect after having been tied to a chair and used as a punching bag for the better part of a day. Some of them had been wreathed in feelings of nostalgia. Some had simply been random.

None of them had involved him waking up covered in his own jizz, heart pounding in the aftermath of a crashing orgasm. This was probably just as well, since he was having enough trouble quashing the occasional daydream about pale marble skin and wild hair the color of a starless night sky.

When he caught those sorts of idle thoughts running through his awareness, he reminded himself very firmly that he was livid with Morpheus, and that he had good reason to be so.

It had taken more than a day before Hugh was up to much of anything beyond popping painkillers like candy and groaning a lot. He knew he'd been lucky to get back to his van in London without attracting the wrong kind of attention.

The drive to his cottage had been terrible, his ribs screaming every time the van's aging suspension jounced over a pothole. Baphometh had eyed him up and down, meowed to be fed, and then fucked off into the forest with an air of disdain. Hugh had reclaimed his own bed, angry and hurt enough by that point not to be distracted by memories of Morpheus' naked form writhing among the plain cotton sheets.

Inevitably, his immortal constitution had knitted his various injuries back together in fairly short order. When he no longer felt like he'd been flattened by a double-decker bus, he went looking for news reports about what had happened in the shop. Apparently, either the news outlets weren't interested in four people going mad in the back rooms of a paranormal artifacts store—complete with a blood-spattered interrogation chair—or else someone had buried the story before it could get out.

That left Hugh at a bit of a dead end. He'd been trying not to think about Philomena and Culpepper's fates, just like he'd been trying not to think about Morpheus' cryptic words regarding stripping power from Iridaceae. Doing so made a red haze of anger gather around the edges of his vision, and he didn't have anyone conveniently available to shout at.

Still, the end result was that he had no leads left to follow. Phobetor had been on Earth. He'd specifically tracked down the magically etched chains that the military had used to bind Morpheus in the bunker. The background levels of craziness that had been slowly growing over the past eighty years hadn't slowed down now that Morpheus was free. If anything, they'd accelerated.

Hugh might not have found any news about Philomena and Culpepper's fate, but he'd been bombarded by stories about political assassinations, newly discovered death cults, suicide bombers, and a particularly alarming piece about a bloke in Eastern Europe who'd tried to sabotage a nuclear reactor and initiate a core meltdown. Humanity continued to bite and claw at itself like a bag full of angry rats.

Hugh had more perspective on the human condition than most. Given the things he'd seen in centuries past, maybe it was naïve of him to think the blame lay anyplace except within the human heart. But the *feel* of the current chaos was different. It felt like something being, if not imposed from outside, then at least whispered in humanity's ear from another source.

With the exception of anyone else who might be working directly with Phobetor—voluntarily or otherwise—Hugh was pretty sure he was the only person on Earth who knew about the threat that the God of Fear posed to the world.

In the absence of better ideas, he went looking for other acquaintances of both Philomena and Culpepper, hoping one of them might have spoken to someone else about the chains or the man who'd bought them. That was how he'd spent the last several days, and he was getting nowhere with it.

On the seventh day, an owl flew in through Hugh's open window.

He dropped the teacup he'd been holding, yelled "*Fuck!*" when the hot tea spattered over his bare feet, and then hopped around like an idiot trying to see where the owl had landed.

His eyes fell on a slight, human figure sitting on the back of his sofa, her chin resting on a fist as she regarded him in turn.

"Hello," she said quizzically.

"Iridaceae!" Hugh limped over to her, barely resisting the urge to grab her and pull her into a bear hug. "Oh, my god! I've been *so worried!*"

She tilted her head at him, birdlike. "Why?"

Hugh tried to reassemble several puzzle pieces in his head, failed utterly, and settled on saying, "Morpheus. He... said some things. About... draining you?" He swallowed. "I was worried you might be..."

She frowned at him. "You were worried I might be what?"

"Dead," he whispered, abruptly ashamed of himself even as the word slipped out. He hurried onward. "Morpheus had just driven four people insane, and we were shouting at each other — okay, *I* was shouting at *him* — and then he said he'd drained your power so he could get to Earth, and I—"

He cut himself off with a gulp.

She was still staring at him with a furrow etched between her delicate brows. "He *did* drain me to get to the Sublunary. I told him it was all right. You were in trouble, and he needed to help you. So, he stripped my power, and I slept for a few days, and now I'm fine."

"Oh, god," Hugh mumbled weakly, turning to flop down on the couch next to where Iridaceae sat perched on the back.

Her eyes lit with a sort of unholy glee. "You thought he *killed* me? *Really?*"

Hugh scrubbed at his face, deflating. "No. I mean… I was angry at him. He was acting like a wanker, and I…" He trailed off, defeated.

"Some gods might have killed me for power, if they needed it badly enough," Iridaceae said, sobering. "Phobetor would have, if it was the simplest solution." She huffed out a sigh. "Anyway, I'm mad at him, too. He's been really irritating since I woke up—all dour and mopey. It's awful."

Hugh shouldn't have taken any satisfaction at that.

"Has he?" he asked, trying to sound casual.

She shrugged. "Insufferable, yeah. Anyway, he's getting stronger again now that he's back in the Night Lands, so I stole a little of his power to come here and get away from him for a bit."

She flicked a tiny gemstone hanging from a delicate chain around her neck. It jumped and bobbed, glowing from within with a blue light exactly the same shade as Morpheus' eyes. Hugh tore his gaze away from it before that thought could take hold.

"Oh," he said.

"I figured he owes me," she replied. "And it only took a little bit. There isn't nearly as much of me to move around as there is of him."

Hugh tried to wrap his brain around that, and immediately gave it up as a bad job.

"I'm glad you came," he said instead. "And I hate to ask this, but has there been any fresh word about Phobetor in the Night Lands? I know he's up to something—he's got the chains that were used to trap Morpheus here on Earth. But I'm running out of ideas when it comes to tracking him down."

Iridaceae's scowl returned. "You shouldn't be trying to track him down. Didn't you learn anything last time?" When he didn't answer, she shook her head and continued. "More of the oneiri are disappearing. Phobetor is probably luring them away to do his bidding in the Sublunary. That's all I know."

Hugh stilled. "He can do that? Even with Morpheus back in the Night Lands?"

"I said Morpheus is getting stronger," she said. "Not that he's *strong*. Not compared to his brothers."

Hugh caught his own flash of alarm, smothered it, and reminded himself firmly that he was angry with the high-handed prick.

Before he could come up with a suitably neutral-sounding reply, Baphometh padded into the room, wove his way through the shards of shattered teacup on the floor, and jumped on the coffee table.

"*Mreow*," he said, his yellow gaze fixed firmly on Iridaceae, rather than on the human who fed him twice a day.

Iridaceae brightened noticeably. "Oh, yes. Good idea, Baph."

Hugh drew breath to speak, but before he could, the air twisted and Iridaceae was once more an owl. The gem glittered low on her feathered chest, still dangling from its fine gold chain. With a flap of wings, she departed through the same window by which she'd entered, Baphometh leaping to follow her before the breeze of her passing had even faded.

"All right, then," Hugh told the empty room, and went to find a broom and dustpan for the broken teacup.

<hr>

When the pair failed to reappear after an hour, Hugh gave up and went to bed. It was a futile gesture. He'd been getting by lately on sheer bloody-mindedness. That, and stubbornly clinging to the idea that Morpheus was a monster, meaning Hugh was better off without him.

As he'd told Iridaceae, he couldn't truly bring himself to believe it. Not deep down. The revelation that Morpheus hadn't done anything to his familiar that she hadn't freely offered removed one rickety leg from the argument Hugh had been having with himself.

Of *course* he hadn't bloody well hurt her. Morpheus loved Iridaceae with a frightening intensity. Hugh had seen the way he'd cradled the injured owl in his arms as he'd dragged the pair home from that horrible bunker.

Now, he lay staring into the darkness of his bedroom, silently cursing himself blue. He knew he couldn't continue to have sex with a man… a *being*… who ignored his right to make decisions about his own safety and his own life.

He also knew that the ugly scene in Culpepper's shop was far from the first time Morpheus had acted rashly to protect Hugh from physical harm. It had never bothered him before. Hell, he'd mostly been grateful.

And, in fairness, what would Hugh have done if he'd walked into that bunker in 1940 to find Morpheus chained and surrounded by armed soldiers? He'd have tried to get him free, of course. And he probably wouldn't have given too much thought to collateral damage while he was doing it.

Was that any different from what Morpheus had done? Some of those men in the bunker might have known about Phobetor and his plans. They might have had valuable information. Hugh would have mowed them down regardless, given the chance.

He sighed, punched his pillow a few times, rolled over, and froze in place.

A silent and impossibly beautiful form stood next to his bed, looking down at him—pale marble skin glowing faintly in the starlight.

"Hello, Hugh," Morpheus said.

SEVEN

HUGH GAPED AT Morpheus for a couple of seconds, then firmly snapped his jaw shut. *You're still angry at the overbearing bastard,* he reminded himself. *He can't just show up in the middle of the night looking pretty and expect you to let it all go.*

"Oh," he said. "It's you. What the *hell*, Morpheus?"

It occurred to him that Morpheus might be here for Iridaceae, not him. Maybe he'd discovered she'd snuck away to Earth using his stolen power, and he was here to take her back. Maybe—

"You're angry," Morpheus observed.

Hugh shook his head, trying to clear it. "Yes. I'm angry. I am extremely cross with you, because you acted like a wanker and now four humans are insane when they didn't need to be—assuming they're even still alive."

A furrow formed between the dark brows. "I... must apologize for my behavior. However, right now it's vitally important that you accompany me to the Night Lands without delay."

Hugh blinked. "I'm sorry. *What?*"

"The Night Lands. I require your assistance with an urgent matter."

Hugh rewound the events of the past week, deciding that he wasn't crazy, and that this truly didn't make any sense. After having determined that much to his own satisfaction, he asked, "If you needed me in the Night Lands, why didn't you just come to me in my dreams like you usually do?"

Morpheus' frown deepened. "You misunderstand. I require *your* presence there, not your dreaming self. I am asking you to accompany me as a fully conscious being." He gave himself a slight shake, like a dog casting off a moment of confusion. "This involves Phobetor, and it's what you might call an emergency."

Hugh's heart kicked into overdrive at the mention of Morpheus' troublesome brother. The entire situation felt subtly off, though he couldn't put his finger on why. It should come as no surprise that Morpheus was utter shit at making apologies. *Or* that he would automatically assume Hugh would drop everything and come with him when asked, despite the fact that they hadn't spoken since their flaming row a week ago.

But... it wasn't as though Hugh was going to tell him to go to the devil when Morpheus clearly needed his help. He almost asked whether they needed to find Iridaceae before they left. At the last moment, he decided not to.

If Morpheus knew Iridaceae was here and wanted to retrieve her, he'd have said so. And if he *didn't* know she was here, Hugh wasn't in a hurry to get her in trouble with her master.

"Uh... all right," he said. "Do I need to get changed first or —"

Morpheus' hand closed around Hugh's arm. Reality spun into chaos with the force of a tornado, ripping at him. Hugh gasped, his lungs inhaling thick nothingness. But before he could properly panic, everything settled and he found himself in a dim cavern, reeling in his companion's grip.

As the dizziness cleared enough for him to remain upright under his own steam, he whirled to demand what the fuck Morpheus thought he was playing at.

The person gripping his arm... wasn't Morpheus.

A young man with perfect, haughty features topped by a riot of golden curls stood sneering at him.

"I'd ask if all humans are so simple-minded and predictable," said Phantasos, "but I already know the answer is yes."

A sinking feeling of dread settled in Hugh's stomach like a lead weight. He gritted his teeth and tried to jerk his arm free, but he might as well have been pulling against a steel band.

"You," Hugh grated. "What the hell do you want from me? What is this place?"

Phantasos eyed him up and down with disdain. "*I* don't want anything from you, pet." He paused. "Well, except, perhaps, for a moment's entertainment. And as for this place, you may think of it as a convenient prison. Somewhere out of the way, where you won't continue to be constantly underfoot... and where you will be readily accessible as either bait, or a ransom."

Hugh steadied his questionable balance in preparation to throw a kick or a punch—not that physical violence had made much of an impact when he'd kicked the God of Death in the balls in a fifteenth century French prison. Still, that had been on Earth. Maybe he'd have better luck on the gods' home turf.

He'd just shifted his weight onto his right foot when two roiling shadows descended on him from either side, coiling around his arms and legs. He would have fallen to the ground beneath the unexpected assault, but the insubstantial wraiths felt a whole lot more solid than they looked. The two—whatever they were—supported his weight with ease, leaving him thoroughly restrained.

"What are you doing?" Hugh demanded, directing the words to Phantasos since he at least had ears, and the swirling things didn't. "Let me go!"

"I fear you won't be going anywhere for a while, Hugh de Ferrers," Phantasos said airily. "My brother's former oneiri are finding their new employment far more rewarding than their previous situation." He gestured impatiently at one of the creatures. "Come, where are the chains? Let us bind him and be done with it, before your new master arrives and is displeased."

The shadow on Hugh's left roiled like oily vapor, and a worryingly familiar set of glowing metal shackles erupted from inside it. Phantasos snatched them neatly away from the creature, and Hugh barely had time to think *oh, fuck.*

He struggled and cursed as Phantasos snapped one thick cuff around Hugh's right wrist, then repeated the action on the left wrist. The creatures—*oneiri?*—jerked him roughly down onto his knees. Before Hugh could shift his center of balance to try and rise again, Phantasos gestured at the chains with one neatly manicured hand.

The free ends seemed to melt into the cave floor, fusing to the stone. Hugh growled as Phantasos took the final item—the collar—and snapped it around his neck. A moment later, it, too, was fastened to the smooth stone floor.

Panic fluttered at Hugh's lungs as he remembered Morpheus bound in this same cramped position, kneeling awkwardly, unable to fully straighten up. That ember of panic flared into an inferno as a new presence entered the cave with a sound like the rustle of bare branches in winter.

Hugh had been bound with his back facing the entrance. He couldn't crane around far enough to see the newcomer, but his shoulders prickled with a prey animal's awareness of an approaching predator.

It wasn't a surprise when Phobetor drifted into his field of vision, looking down his beaky nose at Hugh with disdain shining from his catlike green eyes.

Hugh's mouth felt as dry as the dusty stone beneath his hands and knees. It took every bit of courage in him to stare into that hateful face and speak. "If you're trying to get to Morpheus through me, it won't work. He doesn't want anything to do with me."

Hugh's mind gibbered at him to stop trying to convince his captor that he was worthless, like a bloody idiot. And, okay, that probably hadn't been a smart move…whether or not it was even true.

Phobetor looked from Hugh to Phantasos. "Why is this human still bleating?" he asked, in his voice like dry twigs. He waved a skeletal hand toward the oneiri, which were still hovering nearby like floating oil slicks. "Frighten it, you useless creatures."

Hugh drew breath to say that he was plenty frightened enough already, thank you very much. But then the oneiri descended on him, and what emerged instead was a scream.

EIGHT

IRIDACEAE GENERALLY preferred hunting mice and voles to frogs—but every once in a while, one had a craving. Tonight, the small, squishy creatures living in the stream had been singing particularly loudly, and Baphometh had wanted one—so she'd indulged. Belly full, she flew back to Hugh's familiar cottage with Baphometh scampering after her through the woods.

She would need to return to the Night Lands before her presence was missed. Perhaps it would have made more sense to depart directly after her successful hunt, but Baphometh was good company, and she'd become oddly fond of Hugh over the weeks she'd been trapped with him in owl form.

With luck, the human was done being tiresome about his lover's tiff with Morpheus. She'd like a chance to say goodbye without him having emotions all over her.

He'd left the window conveniently open for them, which was nice. The inside of the little structure was eerily quiet, and it occurred to her that he might have gone to sleep. She alit on the sagging sofa and shifted form, remembering at the last moment to manifest simple clothing.

A soft *scrabble-thump* noise announced Baphometh's arrival through the window. But instead of joining her, he froze where he'd landed, his hackles rising. He made a sound that wasn't quite a growl and wasn't quite a yowl.

Iridaceae frowned. "What is it?" She extended her senses outward, but nothing seemed out of place.

Baphometh shook himself free of his bristly paralysis and ran toward the main bedroom. With a sense of foreboding, Iridaceae grasped the locket around her neck and followed, still scowling.

Hugh lay in his rumpled bed, his body unmoving. Aside from the lack of snoring, this wasn't unusual. At least... not until Baphometh launched his considerable furry bulk onto the bed and started batting at the human's cheek, meowing loudly.

There was no response.

The disquiet in Iridaceae's belly swelled in a way she couldn't realistically blame on the frogs. She'd lived with Hugh for quite a while when Morpheus had been missing, and he was not a heavy sleeper. Not only that, but she couldn't see his chest rising and falling. The nighttime darkness was no impediment to an owl; she should have been able to see the movement.

Baphometh pounced on Hugh's head, grabbing a mouthful of hair and tugging. Still, there was nothing. The cat let out a distressed yowl and leapt to Hugh's chest instead.

Fear tightened Iridaceae's throat. This was wrong. Hugh was immortal. Why was he so still?

"Stay here, Baph," she said. "Watch over him. I'm going to get help."

Baphometh meowed plaintively, curling up on Hugh's chest, over his heart.

It took almost all of the remaining power Iridaceae had stolen to fly back to Morpheus' palace in the Night Lands. He was where she expected to find him—among the walls of mirrors, still sulking.

Swooping in at speed, she transformed as she landed, the shift so abrupt that she stumbled forward a step beforc righting herself.

"Something's wrong with Hugh!" she blurted without preamble.

Her master's sharp blue gaze fell on her, its weight pinning her in place. "I beg your pardon?"

She flapped her hands in frustration. "Your human! Something's wrong with him. He's not moving, and I don't think he's breathing, and Baphometh seems really upset! You need to go and fix him!"

That unblinking gaze never wavered, though Morpheus' shoulders stiffened a fraction. "Stop," he said. "Begin again. How could you know this, when Hugh resides in the Sublunary?"

Iridaceae gritted her teeth and snapped the slender chain looped around her neck, letting the tiny sapphire swing from her fingers. Her guts squirmed with discomfort. Eating all those frogs had definitely been a mistake.

Still, there was nothing else for it. "You were being depressing, so I leeched some of your power and put it in this gemstone. That way, I could go to the Sublunary and get away from you for a bit." She lifted her chin defiantly. "I went to visit Hugh, but he was being nearly as bad as you are, so Baphometh and I went on a hunt instead. When we got back, he was in his bed, not moving!"

Morpheus' brows drew together. "It is nighttime in England. Doubtless he was merely sleeping soundly.

Iridaceae clenched her fists. "You're not *listening* to me! Baphometh jumped on his face and pulled his hair, and he didn't even stir! His chest wasn't moving!"

Her master inhaled sharply, drawing himself up to his full height. "Perhaps he was inebriated. He would not be the first human to drink himself unconscious."

Iridaceae swallowed the urge to scream in frustration—but Morpheus had turned his attention to the mirrors.

"It is a simple matter to check on him," he muttered. "If it will put your mind at rest." He shot her a sharp, sidelong glance. "After which, we will discuss the details of you utilizing my power without my permission. The Sublunary is a dangerous place, as we both have ample cause to know."

Iridaceae refused to flinch or cower. Morpheus was not Phobetor. She had no doubt he could come up with some punishment she'd hate—probably something involving tiresome lessons on ethical behavior. But as long as he found out what was wrong with Hugh and fixed it, whatever penance she had to undertake would be worth it.

Morpheus stared at the mirrors, his expression gradually darkening.

"He's not there, is he?" Iridaceae asked.

His attention returned to her, but now there was alarm hidden behind his gaze.

———————◆———————

Morpheus stretched his awareness outward. The golden thread that should have led unerringly through the chaos of dreamers was gone. For a human, that could mean only one thing. Rage flowed through his veins as possible explanations presented themselves, doing nothing to crowd out the dizzying apprehension constricting his lungs.

Unacceptable.

The entire point of cutting off his ill-considered tryst with Hugh de Ferrers had been to prevent this feeling of utter helplessness in the face of the human's rash and dangerous behavior. It was simple logic. If Hugh was no longer his lover, then his value to Morpheus' enemies disappeared.

Should have disappeared.

"Wait for me here," he commanded Iridaceae, and swept out of the throne room in a swirl of black.

The realm of dreams and nightmares resided between Thanatus' realm of death, Phobetor's realm of fear, and Phantasos' realm of fantasy. He had access to the places where they overlapped, even if he could not penetrate any deeper into another god's realm unless they allowed it.

That had been one of the greatest slights perpetrated against Morpheus in his absence. With his realm's defenses nonexistent, his brother Phobetor had trespassed deep into his lands, seducing the darker oneiri into forsaking their duties and accompanying him to the Sublunary.

Such an incursion was unheard of in the Night Lands. And yet, had he been strong enough, at that moment Morpheus would have stormed Phobetor's territory and cheerfully strangled the God of Fear with his bare hands — brother or no.

He was not nearly that strong. Would not have been, even at the height of his power.

Therefore, he stormed into the borderlands between his realm and his uncle's, rather than trying to confront Phobetor. Dementia. Amnesia. Unconsciousness and coma. When he reached the back wall of the Cave of Hypnos, which he had once wagered on the fortitude of the very same human who had now been ripped from him, he called out.

"Thanatus! Face me!" His voice resonated through the stone, ringing like a bell… spreading outward in ripples.

By rights, the God of Death could have ignored him. Morpheus suspected it was only the unusual nature of his appearance at Thanatus' metaphorical gates that drew his uncle out to see what was going on. Within minutes, a swirl of vaporous darkness seeped through the stone wall of the echoing cave, coalescing into a familiar dark-skinned form.

"Uncle," Morpheus said between gritted teeth. "You have broken a vow you made to me. *I will know why.*"

The hint of curiosity that had tinged Thanatus' features upon his arrival hardened into ice at Morpheus' words.

"Nephew," he said coldly. "I am unaccustomed to being summoned from my work, only to be confronted in such a disrespectful tone. Have a care."

"Hugh de Ferrers is gone from the Sublunary." Morpheus made no effort to moderate the tone that had so offended his uncle. *"Explain yourself."*

Thanatus only stared at him, his heavy brows drawing together. "Who?"

That was enough to break Morpheus' stride—but only for an instant. Had his uncle forsaken his word without even knowing Hugh's *name*?

"Hugh de Ferrers," he repeated slowly. "The human peasant to whom you granted immortality after I won our bet. You agreed to withhold death from him unless he explicitly asked for it."

An unpleasant sinking sensation set up residence in Morpheus stomach. Thanatus continued to glare at him in apparent incomprehension.

"He… he *didn't* ask for it, did he?" The words were wrenched from him without his conscious volition.

"I have absolutely no idea what you're blathering on about, Morpheus," Thanatus said. Then he blinked, a martial light kindling behind his dark gaze. "No… wait. Do you mean the human who spat on me a few hundred years back?"

"The very same," Morpheus said tightly, choosing not to add that Hugh was also the human who'd attempted to kick him in the testicles during that same ill-fated meeting. "He is gone from the mortal world. Ergo, you took him, in violation of our agreement."

That earlier hint of curiosity returned to Thanatus' expression, though it was largely hidden behind the mask of cold outrage.

"I assure you, I did not. Nor do I appreciate the implication, Nephew."

Morpheus took half a step back, mentally calculating the likelihood of his uncle having reaped Hugh inadvertently. Now that his vision wasn't clouded by rage, it seemed staggeringly unlikely.

"But… if Hugh is not in Tartarus," he began, "and if he is not in the Sublunary—then… where is he?"

NINE

"THE ONLY ANSWER I care to give you is that your insolent human champion is *not here*," Thanatus said, with the air of one whose patience had been low to start with—and was now completely exhausted. "Good day, Nephew."

The God of Death disappeared in much the same way he'd arrived, dissipating into a swirl of darkness and flowing through cracks in the cavern wall. Morpheus stood unmoving inside the Cave of Hypnos, alone with his roiling thoughts.

Hugh was not dead, if Thanatus was to be believed. Nor did his soul reside within the tapestry of the collective unconscious. Phobetor was unlikely to respond to Morpheus' summons, assuming he was even in the Night Lands to begin with. These days, his elder brother showed an alarming preference for the Sublunary, and Morpheus was not so flush with power that he dared try to confront Phobetor there.

That left one option for extracting answers.

Morpheus swept across the breadth of his lands in a towering rage, landing in the borderland of Daydreams that separated the realm of Oneiromancy from the realm of Fantasy. He was not entirely surprised to find his younger brother waiting for him there, reclining on a chaise among the threads of mortals' passing fancies.

"Phantasos," Morpheus said coldly.

His brother did not rise, his only acknowledgement of Morpheus' presence the sly smile that played about his sensuous lips. Morpheus stepped closer until he was looming over the chaise.

As his shadow blotted out the sun, it stretched and twisted unnaturally, becoming monstrous. Phantasos — visibly unimpressed by the theatrics — finally deigned to look up.

"Oh, hello, Brother," he said, affecting a tone of boredom. "Fancy seeing you here. Would you mind moving a step to the left? You're blocking my light."

The kingdom of dreams and the kingdom of fantasy were more closely aligned than any of the other realms abutting Morpheus' domain, and yet Morpheus had never felt that he understood his sibling in the least. Phantasos had always been constitutionally incapable of taking anything seriously. He was vain. He was shallow. He did not place sufficient weight on his duties to the mortals, in Morpheus' view.

"Hugh de Ferrers," Morpheus ground out. "Tell me what has become of him, or —"

Phantasos blinked up at him, golden lashes sweeping against his cheeks. "Or?" he echoed innocently.

Morpheus clenched his jaw, the knowledge that he was not even sufficiently powerful to cow his younger brother into compliance burning like acid in his gut. When the impotent silence stretched too long, Phantasos' smile widened into an expression of wicked glee.

"Oh, *dear*," said the God of Fantasy. "Have you mislaid your pet human? How terribly embarrassing for you."

Morpheus glared. "I have no patience for your games, Phantasos. One cannot mislay what has been stolen."

Phantasos laughed. "How interesting. You know, you should have heard the things your little bird said while you were gone. It was enough to make a person question your sanity, Brother. Friends with a human? What kind of folly is that?"

"Says the one who dallies with mortals and discards them like unwanted playing cards at the gambling table," Morpheus replied, unable to help himself.

Phantasos scoffed. "That's rather the point, dear brother. You use them *and then you discard them.* You don't make pets out of them and keep them around for hundreds of years." He lifted his chin, preening. "The foolish creature is completely calf-eyed for you, you realize—Nox alone knows why. When Iridaceae dragged me to the Sublunary to visit him, he thought I was you." His head cocked. "You know, I believe that may be the first time in the history of sentient life that you've been anyone's fantasy. *Ever.* Is that the appeal?"

Morpheus' eyes narrowed, something dangerous kindling inside him at the image of Hugh being deceived in such a way.

Phantasos noticed the shift. His innocent smile turned vicious. "What a shame to be so gullible. Him, I mean—not you. Just imagine how that kind of naivete might be turned against a mortal."

With those words, several things slotted neatly into place in Morpheus' mind with a nearly audible series of clicks. His breath caught.

"This discussion isn't over, Brother," he said, and stormed away before Phantasos could rally a parting shot.

Back in his throne room, Morpheus paced. "Tell me again what happened when you lured Phantasos to the Sublunary," he demanded, not slowing his restless movement.

Iridaceae followed his progress, swiveling her head back and forth in her usual birdlike way. "I was trapped as an owl. I couldn't communicate with anyone here, and I couldn't get back to Earth. I bribed him with pretty baubles until he finally allowed me access to enough power to shift form, and after that I gained his trust by acting as his spy."

"Yes, yes," Morpheus said. "But when he finally took you to Hugh... the details, please."

His familiar shrugged. "You know how your brother is about these things. He must not have been expecting it, but when Hugh woke up and saw us, his mind made Phantasos look like you. Phantasos realized what had happened and started laughing. He said something about Hugh *'having it bad'* and transformed back to his usual appearance."

His jaw tightened. "And Hugh believed him to be me?"

"Yes, as far as I could tell. Though Hugh's fantasy version of you is much prettier than what you actually look like," she added helpfully.

Morpheus stopped in front of his throne and dropped into it. "He believed it was me," he said again, not addressing the words to anyone in particular. "They're in it together."

Iridaceae hesitated, then asked, "Who's in what together?"

Morpheus waved a hand, still sorting out his thoughts. "Phantasos taunted me, implying that Hugh's gullibility would make him easy to manipulate. But Phantasos has no reason to wish Hugh harm. Phobetor, by contrast, *does*."

"You think Phantasos tricked Hugh to get him into Phobetor's clutches," Iridaceae said, making it a statement rather than a question.

"They will be keeping his soul in the borderlands of Hallucination." He rose again, unable to sit still.

"Are you sure?" Iridaceae asked, frowning. "Wouldn't Phobetor want him in the heart of his lands? His palace, maybe? He *does* have dungeons — or at least, that's what people say."

But Morpheus was as certain of his conclusion as he'd ever been of anything in his long existence. "No. If Phantasos abducted him, he would have taken Hugh someplace where both he and Phobetor have access. And the border between their realms is best protected from me. I cannot approach it from either direction as long as they block me from their domains."

Iridaceae crossed her arms, looking flustered. "If they ripped Hugh's entire soul away, it would have killed his body. That's why he wasn't breathing."

"He is immortal," Morpheus said tightly. "Assuming my uncle has, in fact, held to his word — and

I believe he has, based on his reaction when I spoke to him. If Hugh's soul returns, his corporeal form will repair itself."

"But you just said you can't get to him," his familiar pointed out.

And that was the crux of things, was it not? He could see only one way forward. He chose not to dwell on the foolhardiness of what he was scheming.

"Explain what you did to visit the Sublunary without me." He gestured at the tiny sapphire still dangling from its gold chain in Iridaceae's white-knuckled grip.

Her cheeks flushed pink, but she lifted her chin defiantly.

"The last time you gave me power, I pulled a little extra and directed it into this gem to store it," she said, lifting the offending item.

He nodded slowly. "Clever. And in doing so, you have given me an idea. Perhaps I cannot reach Hallucination from within the Night Lands, but there is no reason I cannot do so in the way of mortal things, from the Sublunary."

"You're not mortal, though," Iridaceae pointed out, with some alarm.

"No," he said. "I am not. Come along. I find myself in need of a much more capacious gemstone."

TEN

"THERE USED TO BE more here." Morpheus examined the pile of dream-treasure with furrowed brows, taking in the absence of many of the most striking and valuable pieces.

Iridaceae looked sour. "That's how I bribed Phantasos to take me on when I was stuck here as an owl. He likes shiny baubles."

"He always has," Morpheus said. "And if that is the case, it was treasure well spent. Fortunately, the shiniest objects are not always the most powerful."

He plucked a large black opal from the pile of lesser semi-precious gems. At first glance, it was not an extraordinary stone. Only upon closer inspection did the dark exterior reveal its coruscation of interior rainbow sparkles, like a night sky of stars and nebulae rendered in technicolor.

Opal was not a crystalline mineral, but rather an amorphous mineraloid. As such, it lacked the limitations of a faceted gem, with its myriad tiny reflective mirrors bounding and confining the interior space. Morpheus allowed his mind to explore the depth and breadth of the opal's limits through non-Euclidean dimensions... and was pleased by what he found.

He held the stone up between thumb and forefinger so Iridaceae could see it. "Interesting. A Yuwaalaraay elder in Australia had a vision of the Dreamtime, when the great crocodile Gurria died beneath the supreme spirit Bhiamie's spear. A rainbow descended from the sky, turning Gurria's scales into opals. This was one of the scales from his back."

Iridaceae stared at the opal intently. "It's much bigger than it looks, isn't it?"

"Much," he agreed. After returning to his examination of the remaining pile of treasure, he picked out a second, smaller opal—this one the color of pale, lavender-tinted moonlight.

"Why do you need two?" Iridaceae asked.

Morpheus focused his power and created a setting for the smaller gem, along with a slender chain. "This one is for you. I will not see you helpless in my absence yet again. We will fill this with enough power for you to return freely to the Night Lands and maintain your form as you see fit."

"In your absence," Iridaceae echoed flatly. "You're really doing this, then?"

"It's the most straightforward way to reach Hugh and free him." Morpheus grasped the pale opal and channeled as much of his hard-won power into it as he dared.

Iridaceae accepted the necklace and gave a hesitant nod. "I suppose so. You're *sure* that Phobetor is holding him in Hallucination?"

"As much as I may be." Morpheus crafted a setting and chain for the black opal, hanging it around his neck. It nestled against his chest, thrumming with potential. He gestured for Iridaceae to turn her back and fastened the clasp of her smaller white opal at her nape.

"So, you're going to make yourself into a mortal by channeling all your power into that stone and…

then what?" Iridaceae turned to look at him over her shoulder. "Once you're mortal, how will you actually reach him?"

Morpheus huffed a breath through his nose. "That part is no great feat. Humans have been devising ways to twist their minds free of the Sublunary for thousands of years. I have no doubt one or more suitable substances for achieving hallucinations may be acquired with little effort."

Indeed, once he was prepared to depart, the greatest challenge lay in finding a purveyor of humanity's forbidden substances located physically close enough to Hugh's cottage for convenience. Even after more than a week of recovery in the Night Lands, Morpheus remained far weaker than he would have liked. After gifting Iridaceae yet more of his power, he could not afford to squander what was left on unnecessary travel.

Eventually, he teased free the mind of a troubled young human near the southwestern edge of London's great metropolitan area; one whose mind churned with fears of arrest by the authorities and violence at the hands of other drug dealers.

"It is time to depart," he told Iridaceae, gathering up both the thread of the human's sleeping mind and his faithful familiar.

He dragged them through the ether, piercing the veil separating where he was and where he needed to be with some difficulty. He was *so weary* of this feeling that everything took far more effort than it should.

Unbidden, a flash of memory assaulted him. He was lying on a modest bed, in a modest cottage, where a modest human man held him in place gently by the throat, worshipping him with loving touch and words of awe. Morpheus stilled, closing his eyes for a brief moment.

Such things were not his for the taking. Those had been extraordinary circumstances. His purpose here was to retrieve Hugh from captivity and see him safely home. That was all. If anything, the current crisis only underlined the amount of danger Morpheus had already brought to Hugh's doorstep through their association. Perhaps after this, he could convince the man to disappear and reinvent himself somewhere far away, as he'd already done so many times across the centuries.

Or perhaps after his ordeal, Hugh would make that decision on his own. Morpheus had no illusions. Phobetor would ruthlessly exploit the weakness of Hugh's inexplicable attachment to him. Hugh might well hate the sight of him after being the subject of Phobetor's tender mercies for the better part of a day.

"Morpheus?" Iridaceae asked, tugging on his sleeve.

He sighed and shook himself free of his reverie. "It's nothing. Come. Let me do the talking."

Their target lay huddled on a bare mattress in a filthy bedsit, a threadbare blanket thrown over his body. Clearly, the man was undercharging for his wares… or possibly consuming too much of his own inventory.

He jerked awake with a breathy cry, some awareness of their presence tearing him free of his nightmare.

"What the hell?" Wide, bloodshot eyes in a pale, narrow face stared up at Morpheus and his companion. The human scrabbled backward off the mattress, delving under his sad pile of bedding and coming up with a small knife clutched in one shaking hand. "What the *fuck* are you doing in my room, you arseholes? Get the fuck out before I carve up both your faces!"

Morpheus wasted precious power reaching out to cushion the human's racing mind with sleepy torpor. The hand holding the knife wavered and dipped, coming to rest gently in its owner's lap. The bloodshot eyes blinked up at him groggily.

"I have need of your expertise," Morpheus told him. "I assure you, we pose no danger. I will compensate you well for your time and assistance."

He opened his hand, revealing four gold Krugerrands glinting in the dim light filtering in from the room's single window. That glassy gaze fell on the coins and held there.

The human's mouth opened, hung there for a moment, and closed. "Okay?" he said slowly.

"I need one or more drugs that might reasonably be expected to result in what's colloquially labeled *a bad trip*," Morpheus said. "I should like the experience to last for a minimum of six hours, and up to twenty-four."

The human stared at him.

"Are you for real?" he asked eventually.

Morpheus leaned on his mind a little harder, careful not to send him back into slumber.

The drug dealer's eyes lost focus, turning inward. "Huh. Guess you could try combining LSD with that new distilled salvia tincture. Shit's hardcore. Half the people who take it end up freaking out. Salvia doesn't last for long, but by then the LSD would start kicking in. That stuff can have you tripping balls for up to a day if you take enough."

"Dosage?" Morpheus prompted, lessening his leverage on the disorientated mind now that the human was focused on something other than stabbing them.

The dealer rattled off a series of figures.

"I will purchase twice that much," Morpheus told him, and handed over the gold Krugerrands.

The human gazed down at the shiny coins, bit the edge of one, and shrugged. "I s'pose it's your funeral, mate."

They waited as he climbed to unsteady feet and pottered around the cramped space, coming up with a tiny glass bottle and an even tinier plastic bag with four pills in it.

He put the items in a larger bag. "If I give you this, you'll leave quietly, right? And, like, I'm not responsible if you take this shit and try to jump off a building or something."

"We will leave quietly," Morpheus agreed, taking the bag. "And I bear full responsibility for my usage of these substances."

The man scrubbed a hand over his face. "God, this is fucked up. Shit... am I dreaming this?"

Morpheus let his power wash out, catching the human by the arm and lowering him down to the stained mattress as he crumpled. "Perhaps you are," he said.

Turning to the silent Iridaceae, he gathered her up and wrenched them once more into the liminal spaces beneath the world, emerging in the familiar bedroom of the humble cottage belonging to Hugh de Ferrers.

They were greeted by a startled hiss. Hugh's itinerant cat, Baphometh, sat curled on his master's unmoving chest. His wary yellow eyes blinked as he recognized them, his hackles smoothing.

"He's still not breathing," Iridaceae said in a tone of worry.

Morpheus couldn't completely ignore his jolt of disquiet upon seeing Hugh's lifeless body, but the sight wasn't precisely unexpected.

"Nor will he," he said. "Not until I retrieve his soul."

The cat let out a mournful yowl.

Morpheus drew his shoulders back, steeling himself for what he must do. "Iridaceae—I would ask you to stay and watch over our physical forms. But I must insist that in the event of anything that might place you in physical peril, you will return to the Night Lands immediately."

She frowned. "But... surely if I'm in physical peril, you will be as well. You'll be *mortal*. Do you have any idea how dangerous that is?"

"Return to the Night Lands," he repeated firmly. "Find Thanatus and relay to him everything that has happened."

She didn't look happy, but she nodded reluctant agreement. "Very well."

Mollified, he allowed himself to close the remaining distance to the bed. Baphometh gazed up at him with luminous yellow eyes.

Hugh de Ferrers lay sprawled among the bedclothes in the peculiar disarray that so often accompanied death. Morpheus felt his jaw clench. He resisted the urge to reach out and touch the cold skin. Time was of the essence; sentimentality wasn't useful.

He grasped the pendant at his throat and turned his focus inward. This was not the first time that a divine being had temporarily shed their divinity for some purpose or another. However, previous occurrences had seldom gone well for anyone involved.

But this was the man who had rescued Morpheus from his captors against all odds, despite having no reason to wish to see him again after their argument in 1921. Morpheus could do no less now that their positions were reversed.

The opal absorbed Morpheus' godhood, expanding to accept it like a lake accepting rain. It was a terrible sensation, feeling that defining part of himself draining away—even though it still lay nestled safely against his chest… separate but close by. Iridaceae made a noise of distress, doubtless feeling the loss through their connection.

It was a different feeling than the weakness that had beset him during and after his captivity. A more profound loss by far, though his body continued to function as it should. Lungs inflated, blood thrummed through veins and arteries. It was the awareness of what would happen if either of those things were to *stop* that gave him pause.

They would not stop.

His crafted body was young and vital. This venture would take less than a day. Perhaps mere hours. He could set aside these disconcerting feelings for that long.

"You did it," Iridaceae whispered when Morpheus opened his eyes and straightened.

His stomach rumbled. The sensation was very distracting.

"Yes," he agreed. "Now, for the rest."

Four small tablets lay at the bottom of the little clear plastic bag. He shook them onto his palm and swallowed them all at once. The small glass vial was slightly more mysterious, but the cap revealed an eyedropper when unscrewed. The memory of mortals' dreams provided the final clue, and he sucked up a few drops of the tincture, depositing it under his tongue.

It burned the sensitive mucous membranes there, a hint that the active essence had been dissolved in alcohol. Without a word, Morpheus turned and sat on the floor with his back resting against the side of the bed. His newly mortal flesh clamored with a distracting cacophony of physical feedback. He tried with limited success to ignore it as he waited for the cocktail of drugs to make its way through his bloodstream, to the receptors in his all too human brain.

ELEVEN

THE FIRST HINT that Morpheus was slipping into a state of hallucination came when the distracting thrum of his nerves shifted. Hugh's room was uncomfortably chilly — something that would not have registered in Morpheus' awareness before. Now, it raised gooseflesh along his arms and back.

Abruptly, each tiny point of piloerection began to shift and scrabble beneath his skin… ten thousand tiny insects crawling through his epithelium, burrowing new pathways that itched and scraped like miniature razors. With a choked cry, he clawed at his arms, trying to dig his fingernails deep enough to gouge them out.

"Is it working?" Iridaceae's voice sounded grossly distorted, echoing in his ears.

"Yes," he croaked. "Yes, it's working."

A terrible, fathomless presence seeped into the room, its weight smothering. Morpheus imagined he could hear the timbers of the roof groaning under its bulk, cracks spidering through the plaster of the cottage's ceiling. Worse — and painfully familiar — was the unbearable sense that something incomprehensibly vast was preparing to pass judgment, and it had found him wanting.

"Hello, Mother," he whispered, as viscous darkness flooded in through the ever-widening cracks in the ceiling and drowned him.

His mortal heart thudded painfully against his sternum. He was certain that any moment now, it would break through, ripping itself from his chest and spraying the impenetrable blackness with his crimson lifeblood.

Dozens of clawed hands plucked and grabbed at his limbs as he rose on shaky legs and stumbled forward, deeper into the darkness. He knew those claws. An eternity ago, he had fashioned them from the raw stuff of creation to do his bidding.

"*Oneiri*," he muttered. Then, louder, "You *dare* lay hands on your creator?"

For a bare instant, the creatures cringed away. Then they swarmed forward once more. Maniacal cackling filled the darkness.

"Oh, how the mighty have fallen!" one rumbled, in a voice like thunder.

The insects chewing tunnels through his epidermis hadn't stopped in their efforts to flay him from the inside out. It took an effort of will not to fall to the unseen ground and thrash his limbs in unfettered panic.

But Morpheus knew this place in a way no mortal could. The Night Lands, the domain of Nox, had spawned him—long ago in the primordial past. He had watched its evolution over the passage of eons. He knew what lay beyond the curtains, even though his body now resided on the other side of that heavy veil.

"*You are a weak and pathetic thing,*" whispered a voice. It sounded like his own, and he realized an instant later that his lips had moved around the words, forming them without conscious volition. "*Only one thing awaits you in Hallucination.*"

My destruction, he thought, feeling like a marionette controlled by a murderous puppeteer. *And yet, I must go to it.*

The scrabbling insects crept higher through his body, chewing at the flesh of his trachea and esophagus. Trying to break through. Trying to break *free.* When they succeeded, they would erupt from his body like a many-legged wave, spewing from his nose and mouth.

Thump-thump-thump-thump-thump —

His heart pounded violently, still trying to flee the confines of his ribs.

High, giggling laughter assaulted his ears, growing gradually fainter as the source retreated. Morpheus stumbled forward, following the sound. He scratched convulsively at his neck, feeling his fingernails dig deep into tender flesh.

As he walked, the impenetrable darkness gave way to twisting, impossible shapes. Tesseracts and hyperspheres swelled and deflated around him like balloons, shoving themselves through the confines of three dimensions with the sickly sound of tearing membranes. Impossible colors strobed, blinding him with fractal explosions.

He continued to follow the retreating sound of childlike, maniacal laughter. The tiny part of him that retained a shred of objectivity recognized that these oneiri were damaged… dangerously, and perhaps irreparably.

This was not their natural habitat, any more than the Sublunary was. His brother had lured them from the safety of the dreaming realm, and now they were broken. Anger flooded him, driving away some of the horror at his mortal body's unnatural dissolution.

Other trapped souls wailed and danced and screamed in the ever-shifting waves of light and darkness, their fleeting presences hovering just beyond Morpheus' reach. The itching in his throat tore open in a confusion of scrambling insect legs. He collapsed to his knees, retching uncontrollably. A gout of blood splattered on the ground, writhing with tiny, black-carapaced creatures.

Morpheus heaved, trying to expel every insect in his body. His lungs clenched, unable to draw enough air. Through the ringing in his ears, he could barely hear the gleeful laughter of the oneiri as they slipped farther away into the madness.

Before the trail could disappear completely, he shoved himself off the blood-soaked ground and staggered after them — aware that without the sound of their laughter to follow, he would be hopelessly lost in a realm where mortal senses were worse than useless.

Around him, reality tumbled and twisted in incomprehensible swirls.

⸻ ◆ ⸻

Hours passed in the tiny cottage Hugh de Ferrers called home. Iridaceae kept watch over the human's unmoving body and the twitching, gasping form of her master. Baphometh had eventually relinquished his perch on Hugh's lifeless chest in favor of leaping lightly onto her lap. She sat in the room's only chair, idly stroking his ragged, mismatched ears as his purr rumbled soothingly beneath her touch.

Morpheus was firmly trapped in Hallucination, wandering the borderlands of his brothers' realms, Fear and Fantasy. The shimmering black opal at the base of his throat thrummed with restless life—a god's powers leashed inside it.

"I don't like this," she said plaintively, staring at the beads of sweat dotting a pale forehead that had never perspired before. "What if it doesn't work? What if it *does* work, and he decides he wants to stay mortal forever? What if he decides to leave the Night Lands behind?"

"*Mreow,*" said Baphometh, butting his broad head against her fingers in sympathy.

Iridaceae had seen the longing on her master's face as he watched over Hugh's dreams. It was the first time she'd ever known him to wish for something beyond the scope of his function, and it frightened her.

If it had been anyone—any*thing*—other than Hugh, she might have protested. But without the human, Morpheus would still be trapped in his brother's chains, languishing in that horrible underground tomb with rune-inscribed bullets lodged in his heart and shoulder.

Hugh had sheltered Iridaceae when she'd been stuck on Earth, powerless and unable to shift form. He'd rescued Morpheus. He'd made Morpheus *happy,* if only for a few days.

Her master claimed that the liaison with Hugh had been a mistake. Yet, here he sat, risking himself — risking *everything he was* — to rescue the human who'd once rescued *him*.

"I don't understand them," she muttered.

Baphometh wrapped a paw around her wrist and pulled her hand closer, rubbing his furry cheek against her knuckles. His purring intensified, and she slumped back in the chair with a frustrated sigh.

In the next moment, a crash from the front of the cottage had them both leaping from the chair, Baph's claws leaving four parallel scratches across her forearm.

"Check all the rooms," called a rough, male voice. Heavy footsteps clomped through the entryway. "They're in here somewhere."

Morpheus moaned. Baphometh hissed. Before Iridaceae could gather her scattered thoughts and decide what to do, a terrible, familiar chill settled over the room.

"Baph, *run!*" she cried.

The cat bolted for the room's only window, open a few inches at the bottom to let in fresh air. The sash rattled in its frame as the animal squeezed its bulk through an opening slightly too small for it, but Iridaceae could only pray that he made it out. Her entire focus was fixed firmly on the tall, angular figure that had appeared in front of her like a ghost.

Phobetor's all-too-solid hand shot out, fingers closing around her throat as he shoved her backward against the wall. A picture frame rattled loose and crashed to the floor next to her.

"You again," hissed the God of Fear. "I warned you that I'd rip off your wings, little bird."

The bedroom door flew open, a broad-shouldered man blocking the light from the hallway.

"Is that 'im?" asked the same voice that had ordered the rooms checked. "You want us to bind 'im like you said?"

Iridaceae dug her fingers into the unyielding flesh of Phobetor's wrist, trying to gain enough space to draw breath.

"It's him." The god scowled, his profile wavering in Iridaceae's vision as he craned to look over his shoulder at his brother. "What is he doing?"

"Looks like he's tripping balls," said the human.

"No," Phobetor murmured. He sniffed the air, his nostrils flaring. "Not that. There's something else…"

His pale green eyes fixed on the small opal at Iridaceae's throat. Then his gaze sharpened, and he half-turned his body toward Morpheus. In his distraction, his grip on Iridaceae's neck eased incrementally.

She transformed between one heartbeat and the next, slapping her wings in his face and clawing at his wrist with her talons. Phobetor gave an irritated hiss, but she was already free, flapping up to land on a high bookshelf in the far corner of the room.

With a low curse, Phobetor visibly dismissed her in favor of crossing the few steps to the bed. He crouched in front of Morpheus, who twitched and muttered, clearly unaware of the presence looming over him.

Phobetor reached out and drew the gold chain from beneath Morpheus' collar, the heavy opal dangling in his grip. "Well, now," he practically purred. "Whatever do we have here?"

Iridaceae's heart lurched as he jerked it sharply free of Morpheus' neck, the gold links snapping.

"There's been a change of plans, gentlemen," he said in a tone of utter glee. "It appears I will not require your services after all."

Morpheus' godhood swung lightly from his brother's fingers. Iridaceae dove, her entire focus on wresting it free from him and flying away to safety. Glowing green eyes flared in her vision, and the mindless panic of imminent death crashed over her like a tsunami—swamping every single thought except *flee*.

Her wings missed a beat, and without even knowing she'd done it, she pulled on the stored power Morpheus had gifted her. Reappearing in his palace in the Night Lands, she glanced painfully off the back of his throne and tumbled to the ground in a heap.

Hysteria still pounded through her veins, making her vision swim. It retreated slowly as she lay panting on the stone floor, Phobetor left far behind and separated from her by the veil between realms.

It was only as her rational thoughts reassembled themselves that a fresh kind of queasy dread replaced the God of Fear's unnatural curse of terror.

She'd left Hugh and Morpheus alone with Phobetor. The dead body of an immortal man, and the living body of a mortal one, completely within his power.

Defenseless.

TWELVE

THE ONEIRI LED Morpheus toward the cave that contained the spring of Mnemosyne. With the recognition of that landmark, he once more knew where he was in relation to his own realm, and the realms of his brothers.

The River Lethe, which ran along the border of Morpheus' lands and the realm of Tartarus, was a place of forgetting. By contrast, the waters of Mnemosyne were a well of chaotic memories—and where they entered the edges of Hallucination, the past became fodder for delirium and delusion within the mortal mind.

This, then, was where Phobetor had trapped Hugh. What better torture for a human granted immortality, whose long life was rife with memories of war and loss?

Soul-deep anger lifted Morpheus' awareness above the chaos of insanity surrounding him. Ignoring the unreality of what was being done to his perception of a body, he trudged toward the cavern that he had visited many times over the eons, in the time before he and his brothers' constant abrasiveness had erupted into open contempt.

The oneiri he'd been following swirled around the entrance, guarding whatever lay beyond.

"*Leave,*" he told them.

The maniacal cackling grew louder. Clawed hands reached for him from the churning mass of shadow. Morpheus channeled his visions of the blinding, strobing kaleidoscope that had pierced his eyelids during the journey here. The unhinged laughter turned to screams as the nightmares encountered one thing sure to banish them — the light of day.

Once they were gone, he blinked away the geometric afterimages that sparked and danced in his vision. Ducking beneath the low entrance, he emerged inside the cavern.

As expected, Hugh de Ferrers crouched sobbing and hyperventilating in the center of the echoing space. Glowing metal shackles — all too familiar — encircled the human's wrists and throat, their chains binding him to the living stone of the cave floor. Behind him gurgled the dangerous waters of the spring.

Morpheus refused to acknowledge the way his chest clenched and spasmed at the sight of Sisyphus' inescapable chains. Left to his own devices, Hugh would have been trapped here for eternity — or until his captors found a better use for him and set him free.

But Phobetor and Phantasos had been foolish to hide him away in *Hallucination*, of all places... as though Morpheus didn't know how to make use of his surroundings within the Night Lands, even in his current diminished form. He focused on the chains, remembering the feel of their icy bite against his skin. Remembering the despair, the *desperation* he'd felt in his underground prison as the bombs began to fall in 1940.

Around him, the natural stone of the cavern morphed into concrete and steel, beams creaking and rubble crashing as the structure gave way beneath the Germans' aerial assault. Dust choked Morpheus' lungs. His eyes watered as a figure in a white lab coat came rushing toward him with a golden key clutched in its hand.

I'm sorry, cried the ghost of Frederick Rainey. *I'm so sorry, demon! I'll release you… you can go back to wherever you came fr —*

A steel beam screamed under the strain and collapsed, crushing the soft-spoken scientist. A small, golden key skidded free from his grip, coming to rest a few inches from fingers that spasmed convulsively and then went still.

Morpheus tore himself free of the vision and stepped forward, reaching down to scoop up the glinting bit of metal. The screams and crashes of a bunker buster bomb attack faded into the background.

"Hugh," Morpheus said, crouching before the chained figure. Red-rimmed eyes the color of fresh-turned earth looked straight through him for a moment, before slowly focusing on his face.

Hugh cringed away as far as the chains would allow, shaking his head violently back and forth. "N-no. You aren't him. It isn't real! He… he wouldn't—"

Morpheus couldn't allow himself to think about what sorts of things his brother might have done to torment Hugh's captive soul. He ignored the terrified babble, grabbing the nearest cuff and jamming the key into the lock. With a hard twist, the shackle popped open, and Morpheus threw it aside.

He repeated the action on the metal collar. Hugh scrabbled away from him with a gasp, still constrained by the second wrist shackle. Gritting his teeth, Morpheus grasped him firmly by the forearm before releasing the last of his bonds, holding tight as the human attempted to jerk away from him and flee.

"Let me go... *let me go!*" Hugh gasped. "It's not really you! You wouldn't do those things! *You wouldn't!*"

Morpheus hardened his aching heart, searching for something that would render his companion docile enough to follow him back through the realm of delusions without a struggle.

"You are correct," he said, pitching his voice as calm and steady as he could make it. "It was all a trick. My brothers have been treating you poorly, my huntsman. But now, you must come with me. Agnes needs you. She birthed you a healthy daughter, and she's asking for you. Quickly now... come and see them both."

Hugh's struggles subsided. His bloodshot eyes—swollen from frantic weeping—fell on Morpheus with a look of fragile, desperate hope. "A... daughter? I have a daughter?" He licked his lips. "But... I went to the smithy this morning. Agnes said the baby wouldn't come yet."

"She was mistaken," Morpheus said. "Come with me—I will take you to them. We can go through the woods; it will be faster."

"But the woods are haunted," Hugh whispered, leaning back in alarm.

"The ghosts are not real," Morpheus told him. "I will lead the way. Follow me and try to ignore them. They cannot harm you. Remember, your family is waiting. We must get you to them as quickly as possible."

Hugh gave a reluctant nod and allowed Morpheus to pull him to unsteady feet. Morpheus slid his grip down to tangle his fingers with the human's rather than grasping him by the wrist.

Taking a deep breath that swirled around his face in shining, crystalline fractals, Morpheus led him toward the cave entrance... and into the madness beyond.

Any other human might have panicked and torn free, running for safety that didn't exist. But his champion against Death had no thought for anything beyond the cruel lie of hope that Morpheus had told him. Morpheus retraced his earlier path, returning them to the edge of Hallucination as more visions of unreality danced around them.

When the landscape in front of them finally quieted into still, impenetrable darkness, Morpheus grasped Hugh by the shoulder and hurled him into the void that lay between the Night Lands and the waking world. The human disappeared with a startled cry, but Morpheus' feet remained rooted in place — the ground swallowing them to the ankles.

It seemed the drugs weren't done with his all-too-mortal body and brain. Resigned, he folded himself into an awkward seated position and let the horrors come as they would. At least Iridaceae could look after Hugh if he revived before Morpheus regained his senses.

When Morpheus finally became aware of something beyond his own mind's imaginings, it was the dull ache of contorted back muscles combined with a terrible, cottony feeling in his mouth and throat.

He groaned, rolling into a sitting position. One shoulder knocked heavily against the edge of the bed frame, a sharp bite of pain that roused him the rest of the way from his stupor. He peeled open gritty eyelids and looked around, disorientated.

It was dark, the room illuminated only by moonlight filtering through the partially opened window. The air was damp and chilly, reminding him unpleasantly of the underground bunker where he'd been held for so many years. A violent shiver wracked him, and he realized that the disconcerting association with his captivity had been further reinforced by the fact that he was naked.

Odd. His clothing had been fashioned in the Night Lands, it was true—but the power locked in the opal should have maintained the garments' form even while he was in his altered mental state.

A rustle of movement in the far corner of the room caught his attention. "Iridaceae?" he rasped.

A deeper shadow resolved into the huddled form of Hugh de Ferrers. The human sat hunched in the tight space between a wall and a bookshelf with his arms wrapped around his knees.

"She's not here. The front door's off its hinges. What the hell happened?" Hugh's voice sounded oddly flat.

"Phantasos tricked you," Morpheus said. A terrible feeling of wrongness had begun to swell in his chest and stomach. "What do you remember?"

"Nothing I want to think about." The reply was harsh. "Why were you unconscious? *What did you do?*"

"My brothers' realms are closed to me." He reached for the chain around his neck, discovering it absent. It must have slipped off at some point during his thrashing and writhing. "I was forced to come after you by way of the mortal realm."

He patted the floor around him, reaching under the bed in search of the pendant. His physical form felt *terrible* — dizzy and weak and aching.

"Where is it?" he muttered.

"Where is what?" Hugh asked.

My opal," Morpheus said, halting his search of the floor in favor of going still, feeling for the thrum of power with his mind instead.

There was… *nothing.*

His lungs tightened with dread, cutting off his breath.

"*What opal?*" Hugh demanded. "Morpheus, talk to me, damn it! What the bloody hell is going on?"

The opal was gone.

The front door's off its hinges, Hugh had said.

Iridaceae wasn't here, and the opal was gone. His mind stuttered over the realization, his heart skipping and racing in a thready beat of gathering panic.

In the event of anything that might place you in physical peril, you will return to the Night Lands imme-diately, he'd commanded Iridaceae.

Clearly, something had happened to make her flee. Someone or something had forced its way into the cottage — an intruder too dangerous for Iridaceae to face alone. And now his opal was missing… the opal that held Morpheus' godhood trapped inside, leaving him mortal and helpless in its absence.

THIRTEEN

IT WAS ABSOLUTELY imperative that Morpheus think logically. Hugh was unlikely to be in a condition to offer substantial assistance. Iridaceae was gone. There was no indication that intruders remained inside the cottage — all was silent beyond the ragged sound of his and Hugh's breathing.

Rationality was Morpheus' default state. He would see to Hugh, and then he would devise a plan for dealing with this situation. His muscles protested as he gingerly rolled onto his knees, grasping the edge of the bed with one shaking hand in preparation to rise.

Something deep in his gut clenched and turned over, heaving. The unpleasant roiling sensation that had been churning in his stomach erupted like Vesuvius, filling his throat and mouth with thin liquid that burned like lava and tasted like bitter poison. Eyes wide and streaming, Morpheus lunged clumsily for the small waste basket that sat next to Hugh's bedside table.

The filthy acid spewed from his mouth in gouts, splattering into the little metal container and sending up a stench that was almost as bad as the taste. Invisible bands of muscle pulsed and spasmed in his abdomen, making it impossible to breathe as his body expelled whatever sewage had so offended it.

His empty lungs burned, panic gripping him as his attempts to fill them ran up against a windpipe that seemed to be welded shut. Sparkling lights dazzled at the edges of his vision, followed by an ever-contracting tunnel of reddish gray nothingness.

Hands grasped his shoulders from behind before he could topple face-first into the trash receptacle. His stomach continued to heave, but no more of the poison surged up his throat.

"*Christ*, Morpheus," Hugh croaked, the voice close by his ear. "What... the *fuck*... did you *do*?"

Unfortunately, Morpheus was in no position to speak. He was still far too focused on dragging in wheezing breaths that whistled through his constricted airway—scorching delicate tissue as they went.

The broad hands stilled. One moved from his shoulder to rest across his forehead. "You're... you're *feverish*. That's... you're a *god*. What the hell is happening right now?"

The terrible, strangulating tightness in his throat began to ease, for all that the remnants of acid still coated it like drying paint.

"Gave up my powers," he managed hoarsely, "so I could reach you through the mortal realm."

Silence fell in the chilly room. It persisted for the duration of four thudding heartbeats, and then was broken by Hugh's creative, heartfelt cursing.

"... ridiculous, pig-headed, infuriating son of a *bitch*!" the human railed, the hand still steadying his shoulder shaking him with enough force that Morpheus' vision swam once more. "What the *fuck* were you *thinking*?"

Hugh hauled him upright, slinging one of Morpheus' arms over his shoulder as he'd done when guiding him out of the destroyed bunker. His vision went dark, consciousness wavering at the sudden change in elevation. Without the human's support, he would have crumpled to the floor in a heap.

As it was, his feet dragged and stumbled as the two of them made their staggering way out of the bedroom and down a familiar hallway. Hugh man-handled him into the bathroom, the sudden light as the incandescent bulbs flared to life stabbing at Morpheus' eyes like an icepick. Hugh shoved him over to the sink and leaned him against it, reaching past him to grab a bright green cup and fill it with water.

"Rinse. Spit." The cup loomed in Morpheus' vision.

He blinked at it stupidly. Awkward silence stretched.

"Right," Hugh said slowly. "You, uh… you just vomited. Mostly bile, from the smell of it. Take a sip of this water, swill it around in your mouth, and spit it into the sink. It'll help with the taste. Then you can try to drink a bit."

Morpheus lifted a hand that shook like a palsy victim's, somehow managing to maneuver the cup to his lips. The water made the taste flare worse for a moment, but when he clumsily spat into the basin, things became incrementally better. He did it again, and then a third time. His body rebelled at the idea of swallowing the water, knowing it would hurt—but he needed to be able to speak in more than a rasping whisper.

He drank. His stomach gave a warning gurgle before subsiding unhappily.

The supporting hands guided him a few steps to the side and turned him to sit on the closed lid of the commode.

Hugh's red-rimmed eyes swam into focus in front of him, even as the echo of his brothers' hallucinatory realm teased the edges of his awareness. His skin felt too hot and too tight. His head pounded in time with his unsteady heartbeat.

An explanation. Hugh had demanded one, and if the human was lucid enough to do so, Morpheus owed it to him. He licked his lips, wincing as the remnants of bitter acid tickled his tongue.

"I needed to reach you in the mortal way," he began, attempting with limited success to regiment his thoughts into some kind of order. "My brothers abducted you to the realm of Hallucination, which is cut off from my domain by theirs. I could not access it from the Night Lands with them on guard against me."

"You said that already," Hugh replied flatly. "So, you accessed it the 'mortal' way. What does that *mean*, though?"

Morpheus worked his jaw, trying to summon enough saliva to overcome the awful cottony feeling. "I transferred my godhood into a pendant—an opal. That left my physical form vulnerable to the effects of hallucinogenic substances, allowing me entrance to the realm where you were being held. I retrieved you, but while my mind was distracted, I foolishly allowed the pendant to be taken. Without it, this body is mortal."

Hugh's expression held a blankness that conveyed his difficulty in taking that information on board.

After a moment, he said, "You put your god powers in a necklace… and someone stole the necklace." He blinked. Once… twice. Then alarm crept into his gaze. "You expected Iridaceae to be here. Did the person who took the pendant take her, too?"

"I ordered her to return to the Night Lands immediately if she was in danger." Morpheus hesitated. "But I have no way to confirm if she did so when the intruders arrived."

"Fuck," Hugh said sharply. "Fucking… *fuck*."

He shook his head violently, pushing up and away from his crouched position in front of Morpheus. His balance wavered as he tried to take a backward step, and he had to catch himself against the vanity.

Morpheus gained enough control over his body's clamoring to remember that Hugh was supposed to be the one in need of care.

"You have survived a great trauma," he said, unsure how the observation would be received. "You must care for your own needs."

Hugh stared at him with an expression of complete incomprehension.

"In my brothers' realm, you appeared understandably distressed," Morpheus tried.

"I'm understandably distressed *now*!" Hugh's voice rose until it was almost a shout.

"And you have also been dead for some time," Morpheus finished.

Hugh closed his eyes as though attempting to master himself. After a moment, he opened them, settling his shoulders and speaking in a calmer tone.

"Firstly, whatever happened to me while I was dead is pretty hazy, and I'm more than happy to keep it that way. And secondly, there's this thing humans do where we avoid focusing on one problem by focusing on a different one. Got pretty good at that skill when I was hauling stretchers across no-man's land during the First World War, with shells and mortars exploding all around."

He sighed. Looked down and pinched the skin on the back of his hand between two fingers before letting it go. Then he came over and picked up Morpheus' hand, repeating the same process. Morpheus flinched back in startlement.

"Dehydration pinch test," Hugh said succinctly. "Both of us need fluids and probably some food. Guess you're going to have to get used to roughing it with the rest of us humans while we get this mess sorted out." He refilled the green cup and thrust it at Morpheus. "Here. Drink this."

Morpheus' stomach had grown queasy again at the mention of food, but he obediently lifted the cup to his lips. He managed two swallows before his body once again rebelled. Hugh must have correctly interpreted his sudden gagging noise, because an instant later, he was being lowered onto his knees, heaving into the porcelain toilet he'd been using as a seat.

His stomach muscles screamed in protest, cramping and aching, and when he finally slumped limply against the commode's dubious support, his throat felt as though it had been slashed from the inside with razor blades.

"Maybe you should tell me what exactly you meant when you said 'hallucinogens'," Hugh said, his voice painfully even.

In a thin croak of a voice, Morpheus told him.

Hugh hesitated for a beat. "Holy shit, Morpheus. This is probably going to be an unpleasant few hours."

The words were lost beneath the sound of a fresh bout of retching.

◆

Iridaceae flapped frantically through the ravines and caverns of Tartarus, dodging the shades that tried to stop her. She needed an audience with Thanatus, and she needed it *now*. Typical that the God of Death was nowhere to be found.

When she finally reached his castle—built directly into the rocky cliffs of Perdition—she darted inside before anyone could stop her. Making for the center of the echoing structure, she flew up into the stone arches that formed the ceiling of the throne room and refused to be drawn back down. It felt as though hours passed before Thanatus finally appeared in a swirl of dark robes, folding himself into his throne with an air of exhaustion.

Iridaceae dove from the rafters, pulling on the power stored in her opal to transform herself the moment her feet touched the ground.

She half fell into a deep bow. "Your Grace, there is an emergency! I require your urgent assistance—"

Thanatus straightened abruptly at her appearance. "Where is your master, little bird? Why do you invade my domain in such a way?"

"My master is trapped on Earth!" she said, refusing to even entertain the idea that Morpheus might be dead, mortal as he now was. "Phobetor has stolen his power! Please, Your Grace—you *must* intervene!"

Thanatus' dark gaze might have been chipped from obsidian. "You think to order me thus? What nonsense is this? *Stolen*, indeed," he scoffed, raising a hand as though he might banish Iridaceae from his realm, or from existence altogether.

Iridaceae cringed, bowing lower. "Phantasos and Phobetor abducted the soul of the immortal human, Hugh de Ferrers, and bound him out of Morpheus' reach. Morpheus believed him to be in the realm of Hallucination, so my master transferred his powers into a pendant and attempted to reach him via the mortal realm."

Thanatus gaped, before thundering, *"He did what?"*

Iridaceae swallowed hard. "While Morpheus was indisposed, Phobetor appeared in the Sublunary and stole the pendant, leaving him trapped as a mortal. I couldn't stop him!"

Thanatus gaped some more. Iridaceae held her breath, waiting for the explosion of anger directed at Phobetor's audacious behavior. Eventually, the God of Death snapped his jaw shut, tendons working beneath his skin.

"That *idiot*," he said, low and dangerous. "To risk something so foolish for a human? And then to place that which cannot be measured under the guard of an *owl*?"

Iridaceae bristled, but the flush of offense was replaced immediately by shame over how useless she'd been against Phobetor's powers.

"Please, O Ruler of Death," she begged. "You *must* come to Morpheus' aid. Surely Phobetor cannot be allowed to behave in such a way."

But Thanatus' demeanor had grown icy. "I see no reason to assist one who behaved so irresponsibly," he said, his voice as hard as the stone of Tartarus' cliffs. "In fact, I think your master deserves exactly what he's getting. Let him stew in his own juices. Nephew or no, some decisions bring consequences."

With that, the master of Tartarus flicked a hand in Iridaceae's direction, sweeping her out of his realm and back to the gates of Morpheus' abandoned palace.

Iridaceae clenched her fists, tilted her head back, and shrieked at the sky in frustration.

FOURTEEN

THE NEXT FEW HOURS were, in fact, some of the most trying of Morpheus' existence. Objectively, perhaps they could not be compared to being trapped in the dark underground horror of the bunker. But the torture of an inscribed bullet lodged in his heart could never have been *fatal*.

There was a terrible vulnerability inherent in mortal flesh. Morpheus had learned — via the medium of Hugh loudly berating him — that by taking a combination of drugs in an amount roughly twice the normal recreational dose, he had endangered himself. Worse, he would now be burdened by violent sickness as his body attempted to purge the metabolic byproducts of the two substances.

It was not the first time his physical form had failed him under duress. It *was* the first time he'd suffered the resulting feedback in the same way a human would. His muscles shook. His heart raced and stuttered, as though threatening to give up the fight to pump blood through his veins. Sweat beaded his skin. He stank, in the way all creatures that perspired stank if they did not constantly wash themselves.

And his stomach… *well*. The less said about his stomach, the better.

At first, he thought the humiliation of requiring Hugh's care when Hugh himself was in need of support would be the worst part. Then, he discovered that stomach sickness was sometimes bi-directional, and he was forced to reassess that assumption.

"This… this is *intolerable*," he wheezed, doubling over as fresh cramps and threatening gurgles overtook him.

Hugh perched on the edge of the bathtub with the air of a medieval peasant and mercenary who'd been more closely involved with human waste than most of his modern counterparts. Even *he* wrinkled his nose at the latest round of appalling intestinal noises, though.

"Don't do drugs, kids," he said, as though speaking to an invisible television audience.

Morpheus glared at him.

Eventually, his traitorous body appeared to run out of disgusting substances with which to torment him. Nonetheless, the hours of rebellion left him feeling wrung out—the prospect of even mild exertion bringing a gray haze to the edges of his vision.

His muscles trembled. His head spun. His gut gave a freshly painful clench, although this time it felt different. It was as though the emptiness he'd experienced after being cut off from the collective unconsciousness for eighty years had returned, but this time it had centered itself firmly in his stomach.

"Feeling sick again?" Hugh asked, with admirable patience.

Morpheus placed a shaking hand over his stomach and shook his head. "I do not… think so. It feels more like a pit now, and less like an active volcano."

Hugh gave a little nod, as though he'd expected the answer. "Time to try food and drink again, in that case. Call me unadventurous, but I'm disinclined to take you to a hospital in case the doctors find anything strange about you."

Morpheus tried to scowl at him, but he suspected the effect was ruined somewhat by his weakness.

"Tea," Hugh said, as though it was the unequivocal answer to some unasked question. "And toast. Christ, it's going to be a royal pain trying to keep the house warm tonight with the door broken."

With that, Hugh exited the bathroom—presumably to make the promised tea and toast. Morpheus contemplated following, before deciding it might be safer to stay where he was in case his sickness returned.

Through an effort of will, he got to his feet and rinsed his face in the sink. He swilled and spat more water in an attempt to remove the taste of bile from his mouth. This time, swallowing a few sips afterward didn't result in another round of vomiting.

He felt scoured, inside and out, his flesh as raw with it as though he'd swallowed sandpaper. Staring at the gaunt, hollow-eyed face in the mirror, Morpheus attempted to tamp down the panic that had only been held at bay by distraction over his body's betrayal.

Iridaceae.

Phobetor.

The opal.

If he allowed himself to dwell on any of it, his stuttering heartbeat might stop completely. Already, his chest was tightening again, his throat closing against the air he required to oxygenate base flesh.

Footsteps entered the room, breaking him free of the smothering horror.

"So, think you can successfully cut ties with the toilet for a bit?" Hugh asked. The human sounded deeply weary, as well he might. "Tea'll be ready in a few minutes, and the toast is in the toaster. Did you know there's a machine specifically designed and marketed to toast bread? What a time to be alive, eh?"

Morpheus *did* know that—if only because the little devices occasionally featured in nightmares about fire and electrocution. The startling part was the realization that he now required things like tea and toast for his continued existence.

He nodded wordlessly and made his careful way toward the door, walking on shaky legs as he used convenient walls and furnishings for support. They sat across from each other at the kitchen table, two gray-faced and ghastly figures sipping tea from chipped mugs and eating buttered toast with sweet spices sprinkled on top.

Hugh devoured his portion. Morpheus nibbled with what he considered warranted caution. His stomach rumbled, rolled once like a ship on a wave, and promptly resumed its impression of a sucking black hole. With the abrupt flip of an invisible switch, the golden bread with its topping of sugar and cinnamon became irresistible.

Morpheus threw caution to the wind and finished it in four bites, washing it down with more tea.

Hugh raised an eyebrow. "Better?"

Morpheus waited a few moments for any catastrophic reaction to occur. None did. "For the moment, it seems so."

Of course, *better* was relative. He still felt shaky and strange. Glimpses of impossible fractals—and the shadows of twisted, grasping hands—still danced in his periphery at odd moments.

"Good." Hugh set his mug down with a clink. "Next question. Is there anything—literally *anything*— we can do right now to fix this situation?"

Morpheus couldn't seem to focus his thoughts well enough to think it through. When he tried, he got only as far as '*Gone... the opal is gone, Iridaceae is gone,*' and then his unhelpful mind looped back before it could take another step forward along the chain of logic. He lifted his eyes, meeting Hugh's gaze helplessly.

The human watched him for a long moment. Then he lifted a hand to rub over his lower face, pulling at the skin. Again, Morpheus was reminded that Hugh was in little better shape than he himself.

"Okay," Hugh said. "Whoever broke in and took the pendant must have known to look for you here, specifically. This cottage is in the middle of nowhere—people don't just stumble across it by chance."

Morpheus leaned on Hugh's logic in the absence of his own. "My brothers. They took you as bait for me, just as I feared might happen."

"And you fell right into the trap." Hugh's hand slid up to rub at his eyes and squeeze the bridge of his nose. "Morpheus, *why*? Why would you do something so... so... *stupid*?"

Morpheus stared at him, unblinking. Refusing to say the words aloud.

You know why.

The silence settled, heavy and cold. Hugh broke it with a hissed breath of frustration through his teeth. "Your brothers. Who are *gods*. Which means they, and the pendant, could be pretty much anywhere in the various realms."

Morpheus gave a reluctant nod, the panic threatening to choke him once more.

"And Iridaceae is probably in the Night Lands," Hugh continued. He paused. "I'm sure she'll make her way back to us as soon as she can. She's good at that."

He kindly didn't point out that the last time, it had taken her nearly eighty years to return. Clammy sweat broke out on Morpheus' palms. He wrapped them reflexively around the faint heat of the slowly cooling mug.

A shiver wracked him. Hugh had been right. The cottage was growing chilly as the day's heat escaped through the broken door. The robe Hugh had thrown over his shoulders in the bathroom was insufficient cover to hold in warmth.

"Bath," Hugh said without preamble, in the same way he'd said '*tea*' earlier. "I smell like a two-day-old corpse, and you smell like stale vomit. Let me prop the front door up as best I can and get the woodstove running. Go start the tub filling, if you like—I assume people dream about turning on hot water taps often enough that you're familiar with the process, Your Almighty Kingship."

Morpheus remembered the indescribable comfort of warm water and kind hands after his imprisonment. He gave a reluctant nod and pushed carefully to his feet, not acknowledging the sarcasm.

At the moment, he was the king of nothing—and they both knew it.

He trudged back to the bathroom on legs that felt ever so slightly steadier than before. Thankfully, the smell of sickness and waste in the air had dissipated until it was merely unpleasant, rather than overpowering.

A brief examination of the bathtub's plumbing revealed it to be relatively straightforward. He plugged the drain hole and experimented with the taps until the water that rushed out was hot enough to prickle the skin of his wrist.

Morpheus was lying back in the steaming water when Hugh reappeared sometime later with a bundle of folded clothing in his arms. He paused, his gaze catching on Morpheus in the bath. After a moment, he wrenched his attention free, set the clothes on the vanity, and withdrew a plastic bottle from one of the cabinets. An aerosolized mist shot from its nozzle, replacing the lingering scent of vomit with a sharp, chemical tang that was probably an improvement.

Morpheus closed his eyes, letting his head fall back to rest against the tub's rim.

Task evidently completed, the human cleared his throat. "There are… uh… some clean clothes here when you're finished. They'll be huge on you, but the track pants have a drawstring. I'll, um, just get you a towel and some soap, and—"

"*Hugh,*" Morpheus said wearily, not opening his eyes. "Take your clothes off and get in the damned bath."

The room went completely still except for the gentle lapping of water against porcelain. Long seconds passed before the rustle of clothing being removed finally broke it. A callused hand urged Morpheus to shift forward, making space, and Hugh got into the damned bath.

FIFTEEN

IRIDACEAE SAT cross-legged on Morpheus' throne, staring unseeing at the ever-shifting images on the mirrored wall in front of her.

She'd been paralyzed by indecision for hours after speaking to Thanatus. Morpheus had ordered her to return to the Night Lands if danger threatened on Earth. She'd done that, but it was clear no help would be forthcoming from anyone powerful enough to stand against Phobetor.

The pale opal still hung at her throat—a heavy weight of responsibility despite its small size.

She thought it retained power enough to transport her back to the Sublunary. It was unlikely to contain enough for a return trip to the Night Lands afterward. What if she went, only to find Morpheus and Hugh dead? She would be as trapped in the mortal world as her master had been when the humans captured him in 1940.

With a birdlike movement of frustration, she shook her head sharply.

It didn't matter. Perhaps there would be enough residual power in the opal to allow her to shift into owl form if Morpheus and Hugh were gone. She could find Baphometh and they would live in the woods together, catching mice and drinking rainwater. That would be a far better life than staying here alone in this place of cold, uncaring gods.

Decision made, she slipped off the throne and reached out for the recently traveled path through the veil… the one that led to the familiar refuge of Hugh de Ferrers' cottage.

———◆———

"You are angry with me." Morpheus lay back in Hugh's loose embrace, the water lapping around them. "That is understandable. I badly misjudged the situation with my brothers."

"You misjudged *something*, that's for sure," Hugh muttered. "I'm just sitting here waiting to see if you have the first clue what it is."

Morpheus drew breath to answer, unsure exactly what words needed to emerge to salve the situation—only to be interrupted by the scrabble of small claws against the closed bathroom door. A muffled meow followed a moment later.

Hugh's muscles tensed behind him at the scratching, only to relax when he recognized the source.

"Oh, good," he said with a sigh, his tone caught somewhere between irony and genuine relief. "The cat's back."

Then the doorknob turned, and Hugh twitched hard enough to send water sloshing over the edge of the bath. Morpheus stiffened as well, abruptly aware that he had no way to sense if the intruder was friend or foe. He had stupidly assumed that they would be safe in the aftermath of Phobetor's attack—

"Hello?" A feminine voice filtered in, and a fresh round of lightheadedness made Morpheus' vision swim, his apprehension draining away as abruptly as it had come. The hinges creaked as Iridaceae eased the door open far enough to poke her head inside. Hugh's scarred excuse for a cat took the chance to dart through the gap and jump up on the toilet seat, surveying them with a beady eye.

Iridaceae blinked at them. "Oh. You're both still alive. That's good. And... you're doing naked things again. *Already?*"

"Iridaceae," Morpheus said, reaching for dignity and grasping the obvious instead. "You were able to return."

"Hullo, luv," Hugh said, sounding resigned to the awkwardness of the situation. "Glad you're okay."

The cat—Baphometh—let out a plaintive yowl as though to echo the sentiment.

Iridaceae's slender shoulders hunched inward. "I ran away when danger threatened you," she said in a tiny voice. "*Again.*"

Morpheus frowned. "You retreated to safety, *as I instructed,*" he said firmly. "Phobetor was the perpetrator, was he not?"

She nodded miserably. "He took your pendant. I couldn't stop him."

Hugh sighed. "Iridaceae, he's a *god*. No one expected you to stop him. You got out of harm's way before he could hurt you. That's all we care about."

"And you came back," Morpheus added, rallying. "You did well; I will tolerate no more self-deprecation."

Iridaceae chewed her lower lip, looking unconvinced. She lifted the pale opal necklace from beneath the neckline of her simple clothing. "I still have this. I don't think it has enough power left to get me back to the Night Lands. Can you use it, though?"

The second pendant had contained only a tiny fraction of his power to begin with. Now, it retained next to nothing.

"No," he told her, as kindly as he could. "You keep it. Were you able to speak to Thanatus?"

Iridaceae's woebegone expression morphed into abrupt, vicious fury. Her lip curled in disgust.

"He won't help," she snarled. "He said—" But then she cut herself off, shaking her head angrily. "It's not important what he said. It wasn't very nice, though. I tried to argue, but he swept me out of his lands and back to your palace. So, I came here."

Morpheus would press the issue of what, exactly, his uncle had said… *later*. Now, the exhaustion that had been pricking at him swelled until he could barely think past it.

"You did well," he said again. "For now, perhaps it would be best if we all got some rest. It has been an exceptionally trying day."

Hugh had been following the exchange without adding anything, but at that, he said, "The couch is yours if you want it, Iridaceae. My bedroom needs a good cleaning before it's fit for habitation, and I'm afraid this one—" He gestured at Morpheus. "—already has dibs on the guest bed. Can you shift form, or are you stuck as a human this time?"

Iridaceae's nose wrinkled. "There's probably enough power left in the necklace to shift into an owl. Not sure there'd be enough to shift back again.

After last time, maybe it's best if I stay like this so we can talk."

"Maybe so," Hugh agreed. "Okay… would you mind taking Baph to the kitchen and getting him some cat food? Help yourself to anything in the fridge if you're hungry. Morpheus and I could use some privacy for a bit."

Iridaceae hesitated, then gave a knowing tap to the side of her nose. "Right. Naked stuff. Got it. Come on, Baph." She jerked her chin toward the doorway, and Baphometh hopped down from his perch. "Let's get food."

The pair retreated from the bathroom, the door closing after them with a firm click.

"Well, that's one less thing to worry about," Hugh said philosophically, slumping back in the tub. "Two, if you count the cat."

"Indeed," Morpheus agreed, still battling light-headedness now that he knew Iridaceae was safe.

"You're trembling." Hugh's tone was flat. "Here, let's scrub off the worst of the stench and get out of this tub before the water gets cold. I suppose we can have a flaming argument about our relation-ship after we've both had a decent kip."

Morpheus accepted Hugh's assistance in wash-ing and drying himself, followed by a detailed demonstration regarding the proper use of a tooth-brush. The aggressively minty flavor of the toothpaste felt like a direct assault on his tongue, but it did finally — *blissfully* — remove the lingering sour-ness of bile.

Afterward, he rallied enough to reach the tiny guest bedroom without Hugh's physical support, since the human's footsteps were dragging almost as badly as his own. When they passed the cozy sitting room, Morpheus glanced in to see Iridaceae curled on the sagging green sofa with a blanket wrapped around her. Baphometh's head poked out from the gap, and a rumbling purr filled the room.

The bed in the guest room was clearly not designed to accommodate two people. Morpheus grasped Hugh by the shoulder and shoved him onto it anyway, slipping in behind him and curling his lanky form around the human's back like a second skin.

Hugh sucked in a startled breath and held it. When it finally shuddered free of his lungs, his whole body shook with it. After a pregnant pause, he covered Morpheus' encircling arm with his, pressing it closer against his body.

"I *do* understand what else I misjudged," Morpheus said softly. He burned with humiliation over the necessity of speaking the words aloud, yet he was unwilling to leave them unsaid. "I will not make that mistake again."

Hugh's chest jerked once, a faint, pained noise squeezing free of his throat before he could catch it. The hand covering his clenched, callused fingers tangling between Morpheus' own to squeeze him tight.

SIXTEEN

IT WAS MORNING. There was a man in Hugh's bed who should have been a god. And the fact that he currently *wasn't* a god might be the only thing allowing Hugh to keep his head on straight after the past few days.

The sun peered grudgingly through the guest room window, as though it, too, had slept poorly. Hugh lay on his side, propped up on an elbow, staring at the gorgeous, completely mortal twink currently drooling on his pillow.

Was this the first time in his long existence that Morpheus had ever slept? Had he dreamed? *Could* he dream?

One thing was certain—he hadn't yet been absent from his realm long enough for dreams to descend into the formless chaos that had defined his long imprisonment in a British military bunker. Hugh's nightmares last night had been *quite* sharply defined, thank you very much.

He knew, intellectually, that Phobetor had played on his darkest fears when he'd been trapped in the realm of hallucination. The *problem* was that Hugh's darkest fears had a certain rational basis in reality.

Morpheus was... if not an outright killer, then at least the sort of being who would coldly manipulate someone into swallowing a bullet as a way to escape being smothered in their own worst nightmares for eternity. Inside the cave, Phobetor's creatures had twisted that purely factual knowledge into a vivid hallucination. One where Morpheus had punished Hugh for defying him by torturing Mary Walthorpe, her entire family, and all their beloved dogs and horses into madness and death while forcing Hugh to watch.

The horrific *wrongness* of it had warred with the tiny corner of Hugh's insecurities that said it wasn't fully outside the realm of possibility. He wasn't proud of the existence of that tiny corner. In the cold light of day, staring down at a skinny bloke with bedhead and drool drying on his chin, he was mostly able to pretend the corner didn't exist.

The Morpheus who had taken too many drugs and ended up puking his guts out in Hugh's toilet was not the same creature who would mete out metaphysical torture to make a point. The Morpheus who had wolfed down tea and cinnamon toast like a starving wolverine was not the same creature who could drown a room in shadows channeled directly from the void, simply because his mood soured.

And right now, that was a good thing... for Hugh's sanity, if nothing else.

The skinny twink who *definitely wasn't* the God of Nightmares winced and stirred into wakefulness with a pained groan. Blue eyes flickered open... still bleary, but less bloodshot than they had been the previous night.

"Good morning," Hugh greeted that unfocused gaze. "How's the head?"

Morpheus looked like someone deeply offended by his body's betrayal. He started to sit up, made another wordless sound of torment, and flopped backward to lie limp on the mattress.

"I'll take that as a 'not great,' then," Hugh said.

Morpheus blinked up at the ceiling for a few moments before appearing to rally.

"I must recover the opal," he rasped. "This situation is untenable."

"Uh-huh," Hugh said. "Sure. And how are you planning on doing that, exactly?"

Blue eyes glared at him. No otherworldly void-shadows followed. Hugh raised his eyebrows in a 'Well?' gesture.

"I do not know," Morpheus admitted, as though the words had been dragged from him.

Hugh nodded. "Yeah, me either. So how about we start with breakfast and paracetamol, and go from there?"

The glare didn't soften, but after several seconds, Morpheus closed his eyes with an unhappy sigh.

"I thought you wished to have an argument first, about..." He trailed off as though the next words had stuck in his throat.

"Our relationship," Hugh said agreeably. "Yes, that's right."

The blue eyes remained closed, faint lines of strain at their corners. "I was angry that you continued to place yourself in harm's way by pursuing information about Phobetor."

Silence settled.

"And?" Hugh prompted.

A tendon worked at the corner of Morpheus' jaw. "I sought to control your actions. When it became apparent I could not, I sought to minimize the danger you were in by severing our association."

Hugh let that settle between them for a moment.

"Was that *really* why you dumped me?" he asked, unable to keep the skepticism from his tone.

At that, Morpheus' eyes flew open, a furrow of confusion crinkling his brow.

"Yes."

And... that reaction had a surprising air of truthfulness to it.

"You weren't trying to punish me for not falling in line like a good little mortal?" he pressed.

"No," Morpheus said, sounding bewildered. The frown deepened, and he hesitated. "That is to say—"

Hugh hauled himself up to rest against the headboard, waiting him out.

Morpheus licked his lips. "I... could not reconcile my fear for your safety with my inability to make you act in a rational manner. One that would keep you safe. Even when I discovered you bound and beaten by Philomena Waldenpole's associates, you seemed less concerned with your own injuries than with my punishment of your captors."

Hugh chewed the inside of his cheek, aware that if they were really going to do this, it meant he'd have to share some uncomfortable truths as well.

"It was the first time I was ever frightened of you," he said reluctantly. "You drove Philomena and Ted Culpepper mad, when all you had to do to get me out of there was send them to sleep."

"And afterward, you accused me of murdering my own familiar to steal her power," Morpheus murmured.

Hugh winced, not entirely sure when he'd ended up on the wrong side of this discussion. "Yes," he admitted. "Not my finest moment. And I am sorry about that part."

"I drove the humans mad because they had harmed you," Morpheus said slowly. "But also, because they had become my brother's creatures. They could not be allowed to report back to him with anything they might have discovered."

Hugh turned the words over, assessing them. "I was angry because they knew things about Phobetor's plans, and that knowledge was lost when you destroyed their minds. I… didn't really think about it from the other direction. Mostly because I don't think they knew anything important that Phobetor didn't know already."

Blue eyes burned holes in him. "And would you be willing to stake your life on that?"

"I'm immortal," Hugh said tiredly. "Which is more than we can say about *you* at the moment."

"*They hurt you.*" The words sounded like sandpaper.

"And you *dumped me*," Hugh shot back. "How was *that* not hurting me?"

Morpheus' jaw snapped shut with a sharp click of teeth.

Silence settled. Stretched.

"That was my mistake," he said, when it finally grew too heavy. "As I have already stated."

Hugh's nerves were vibrating like a plucked violin string.

"Does that mean I can consider myself undumped?" he asked, fighting to keep it light.

"Because, no offense, but I don't usually hold my exes' hair back for them while they're projectile vomiting into my toilet."

Morpheus' expression soured at the reminder of the previous day. "I fear any pretense I might make of emotional distance would not survive close scrutiny."

"Yeah, probably not," Hugh agreed. "Just so long as we're on the same page, then."

"I believe we are." Morpheus swallowed, his throat bobbing. "A fact for which I am thankful, given my current... *difficulties.*"

Something settled in Hugh's chest—a weight off-balance, finally achieving equilibrium.

"Yes," he said. "About that. You need to eat something more substantial than toast. After which, I need to tackle some logistics, like clothes for you and Iridaceae, along with supplies to fix the bloody front door... assuming we're staying here, that is. How likely is Phobetor to come back?"

Angular features twisted. "He has no further reason to return to this place. His goal has already been achieved—my interference has been neutralized. In his mind, I'm sure he considers this a suitable punishment for me."

Hugh sighed. "I know you're talking about your mortality rather than being stuck here in my cottage. So, I'm going to try really hard not to take that personally."

Morpheus did, at least, have the good grace to look sheepish. "Quite."

After shepherding a lost godling through the basics of a morning hygiene routine, followed by a breakfast conjured from cupboards that were nearly bare, Hugh made a comprehensive list of necessities to buy and headed for the nearby town of Sandhurst in his battered van.

For the most part, he preferred to purchase the things he needed from local shops — but there were times when it was more efficient to take advantage of the recent human obsession with so-called 'big box' stores. With food, clothing, and lumber supplies vying for his attention, the Sandhurst shopping mall anchored by a Tesco at one end and a Marks and Spencer at the other was an obvious choice.

He'd donned a disposable mask as a nod to the ongoing pandemic. He was just browsing through a selection of novelty jumpers, trying to decide which ones Morpheus would hate the least, when a *crash-boom-whoosh* echoed from the direction of Kitchenware. A hit of adrenaline leftover from far too many battlefields sent Hugh whirling in the direction of the explosion, even as the first shrill screams of fear reached his ears.

Flames roared, incongruous above the drone of inoffensive piped music. Greasy black smoke rolled along the white ceiling panels. Moments later, a second explosion rocked the store, followed by more screams… closer, this time.

Some instinct — left over from the war that was supposed to have ended all wars — whispered *help the injured.* Heart in throat, Hugh dropped the '*All Aboard the Bipolar Express*' jumper he'd been holding and charged toward the sounds of terror.

SEVENTEEN

THE MAN CAUSING the chaos had a hoodie pulled tight over his head and a kerchief tied around the lower half of his face. The flap of the large messenger bag slung over his shoulder was open, and he pulled out a fresh Molotov cocktail even as he shouted at the cowering shoppers trapped between him and a wall of crackling flames.

"You're all in on it—*every last one of you!*" he ranted, gesturing with a silver cigarette lighter at the small knot of terrified people, some of whom were clutching crying children. "Well, I'm *onto you*, d'you hear me! *I'll burn you all to ashes, and your fuckin' crotch-spawn too!*"

Smoke billowed from shelves of burning bath towels, the fire racing greedily along the length of the aisle. Hugh's head spun, his vision narrowing down to the cigarette lighter as the man flicked it into life. Without stopping to think, Hugh charged the bloke from behind, sending him spinning with the impact. The lighter went arcing away, hitting the floor with a skittering, metallic clink.

Hugh aimed a vicious chop at the hand holding the Molotov cocktail, which shattered at their feet as it fell. Petrol splattered their trouser legs, spreading into a puddle around their feet as they struggled.

"Run... *run!*" he shouted to the horrified on-lookers, but he couldn't spare any attention to make sure they listened.

The arsonist wasn't a big man, but he fought like a rabid hyena—scratching and clawing and kicking. Only meters away, the flames jumped to another set of shelves with a loud whoosh of displaced air.

Hugh slipped on slick petrol, barely managing the presence of mind to use his momentum against his opponent. He dragged the arsonist off balance with him, tangled an ankle between the other man's legs, and took them both down… twisting at the last moment so his opponent absorbed the brunt of the fall.

He landed on his messenger bag to the sound of more shattering glass. Ignoring the twinge of a bruised knee, Hugh grabbed him by the hoodie and slammed a solid right hook into his jaw. The bloke grunted and went limp.

Hugh shoved off him and staggered to his feet, stumbling backward out of the spreading puddle of fuel. Gasping and coughing in the smoke, he continued to backpedal until his shoulders hit a metal shelving unit—fortunately, one that wasn't on fire yet. Decorative bathroom mirrors rattled under the impact, a large one toppling to the floor in an explosion of silver shards to his left.

Startled, Hugh whirled to look at the destruction—*seven years bad luck*, whispered a superstitious little voice in the depths of his mind. When he looked back, it was to see the spreading puddle cross the last few centimeters to the nearest burning soft goods.

Blue flames raced along the floor, reaching the dazed man's petrol-soaked clothing and exploding into an inferno. The figure flailed among the rippling blue and orange conflagration, screaming in agony.

For several seconds, Hugh gaped stupidly at the scene of carnage, his thoughts molasses-slow. The stench of petrol rose from his own shoes and trousers, splattered there liberally when the first bottle had shattered. If he got anywhere near the burning man, he'd go up like a roman candle as well.

In the distance, sirens wailed.

Hugh stared at the writhing arsonist for another endless few seconds, then turned and lurched clumsily toward the front of the store. He coughed and gagged, his eyes streaming. When he reached the sliding glass doors—thankfully propped open—a fire truck was just screeching its way into the parking lot.

Someone tried to grab his arm as he passed through the crowd of people gathered outside, but he jerked free of the grip and made a beeline for his van. His hands shook so badly that it took three tries to get the key in the ignition. The smell of petrol and smoke choked him. He ripped off his disposable plague mask and rolled the window down almost violently, gasping for fresh air.

More sirens approached, lights flashing in the distance. Hugh clutched the steering wheel and the gearshift with a white-knuckled grip to quiet his body's tremors, reversing out of the parking space faster than he should have. Before the police could get organized enough to lock down the car park, he pulled out and onto the road—forcing himself to slow down... not to draw unwanted attention with a squeal of burning rubber.

Stomach roiling, he drove until he came to a stretch of greenspace marked as a nature preserve. He pulled into the first parking area he saw and killed the engine, curling forward until his forehead thumped against the top of the steering wheel.

Maybe it was just a fluke, he tried to tell himself. *Sometimes crazy people snap and do crazy things.*

He knew it was a lie, though. He'd lived through eight hundred years of humanity's thrashing and flailing toward civilization. And he'd seen the slow slide toward chaos in the decades since the God of Dreams had been trapped in a British bunker, leaving the God of Fear free to steal his nightmares away and unleash them on the waking world.

Hugh breathed past his tight throat and tighter chest, picturing Morpheus' likely reaction should he learn of the true state of the world beyond Hugh's remote rural cabin.

Morpheus was *human*.

Phobetor had nearly destroyed him twice already. If Morpheus tried to fight his brother now, he could *die*. For long moments, Hugh sat shuddering... his wheezing gasps sounding loud even with the van window rolled down.

Eventually, he straightened, his decision made.

He pulled out his phone, finding a spidery crack in one corner of the screen. It powered on normally, though... so he pulled up the online map and scouted out the nearest B&Q warehouse. It was only ten minutes away, and the employees would be less likely to throw him out for smelling like a petrol fire than if he tried to go to a regular clothing store.

Girding himself to handle practicalities when all he really wanted to do was sit down in a corner somewhere and rock, he drove south to Farnborough and walked into the home improvement store with the air of a man on a mission.

Several people gave him startled looks when they ventured within his zone of stench, but he ignored them. The only clothing choices were work trousers with huge cargo pockets and sweatshirts with power tool brand names splashed across the chest. He picked something in his size and went through the checkout, flashing the female employee his best self-deprecating smile as she wrinkled her nose in distaste.

"Sorry," he said. "Bit of an accident at the job site, as you can probably smell. Is it all right if I wear these out of the store?" He gestured at the clothes.

"I think that's probably a good plan, mate," said the checkout worker. "Just keep the receipt handy in case someone asks, yeah?"

He thanked her and paid for the clothing, taking his purchases back to the restrooms. After changing in a cubicle and throwing his old clothes in the bin, he ducked his head in one of the sinks and took a stab at rinsing the smell of smoke out of his hair.

Outside, he did a sniff test, his chest catching on an aborted cough. His shoes still smelled of petrol, but it was fading as time went on. Figuring this was about as good as things were going to get in the absence of a shower, he went back to the lumber department and gathered what he'd need to fix the cottage door.

The next stop was a nearby H&M clothing store, since he doubted Iridaceae — or Morpheus, for that matter — would appreciate clothes plastered with bright yellow DEWALT logos. Several customers were shouting at a beleaguered employee in the menswear department as he passed, but Hugh managed to get in and out of the store before anything erupted into physical violence.

The last stop was a grocery store. He joined the crowd of shoppers with tense, hunched shoulders and darting eyes, suspecting that he would fit right in with them. They sped through the aisles with their squeaky trolleys as though expecting highwaymen to descend at any moment and steal their Weetabix at gunpoint.

Hugh's head was throbbing by the time he'd loaded everything into the van and headed for home — whether from smoke inhalation, stress, or a combination of both. His tension didn't ease as he pulled onto his long and winding drive, uncomfortably aware of how many hours he'd been gone, leaving Morpheus and Iridaceae alone and undefended in a cottage with no working front door.

Iridaceae looked up as he entered the kitchen and said, "Oh, good, you're back," in a tone of limited interest. Only then did his shoulders start to relax.

"Where's Morpheus?" Hugh asked.

Iridaceae shrugged. "Sleeping, I think. Must be a novelty for him." Her nose scrunched up. "Why do you smell so disgusting?"

Poker-faced, Hugh met her amber eyes and said, "Some poor bloke's car caught fire on the side of the road. I stopped to make sure he was okay, but things got a bit smokey. And... er... petrol-y."

"Oh," she said. "Okay. Is there food?"

"Yeah, lots. I'll just get it put away, and then go have a shower."

Thanking his lucky stars that Morpheus was apparently making up for a near-eternity's worth of sleep deprivation, Hugh put everything away and got himself cleaned up, dressing in his own clothes rather than continuing his new role as a walking advertisement for drills and circular saws.

When he quietly snuck into the guest room, it was to find Morpheus lying face down on the bed, his slender body swimming in one of Hugh's too-large t-shirts and a pair of drawstring pajama bottoms.

"Hey," he said softly, and was rewarded with one bleary blue eye peeling open to peer at him. "I'm back."

Morpheus blinked, then levered himself onto an elbow. "So you are." He took in Hugh's damp hair and change of clothing. "Is everything all right?"

Hugh made himself smile, reaching out to brush his fingers over a sharp cheekbone.

"Right as rain, love. Come on—up you get. I've got you some clothes that will actually fit your skinny arse, and food to maybe help make it a little less skinny. Afterward, I'll fix the door. Then we'll be set. I think we could all use a bit of a rest."

EIGHTEEN

MORPHEUS LAY IN Hugh's bed, contemplating the idea of *rest*. Four days had passed since his disastrous rescue attempt in the realm of Hallucination, and his mortal body seemed to have largely repaired itself under Hugh's watchful care.

He'd learned the basics of human feeding and hygiene. Painfully awkward and humiliating as the process had been, it was not, ultimately, that complicated. Somehow, the urgency of that first, terrible night had faded. Iridaceae's safe return from the Night Lands had dulled the sharp edge of his initial panic, making it more difficult to remain on high alert.

Morpheus knew he needed to solve the conundrum of his lost godhood—not least so he could confront Phobetor on an even playing field and recover his stolen oneiri. However, the only potential solution that had so far presented itself was distasteful in the extreme. He had not discussed it with Hugh, knowing that doing so would only upset the human and lead to another fight.

Perhaps there was no harm in taking a few days to *rest*, in the quiet way mortals did. Morpheus hadn't expected to find solace in the gentle rhythms of the Sublunary. And yet, as he lay curled on his side beneath the warm blankets, watching the landscape beyond the window shift from darkest night to the gray of predawn, he took pleasure in the presence of the body pressed to his from behind.

Hugh had returned from his expedition to procure clothing and sustenance for them with an air of edginess, but he soon settled into his self-assigned task of repairing the broken front door. Morpheus had watched his easy competence with hammer and saw, occasionally handing him tools when requested. Sometimes, they'd even been the *correct* tools.

His human paramour was a man who took comfort in the use of his hands—in repairing that which was broken, and in improving that which had not yet reached its full potential.

Morpheus wasn't entirely certain into which category he fell. Somehow, he couldn't seem to summon the expected levels of resentment toward either one.

This morning, he was well fed and well rested, for all that he had yet to dream as mortal things did. His physical body was free of pain... only a bit stiff in places, which Hugh assured him was normal after lying in one position for hours.

Moving held little appeal when Hugh's arm lay heavy across his torso—warm breath whuffling softly against the nape of his neck. Indeed, the intimate, almost ticklish sensation was having an odd effect on him, washing shivering heat along his nerves to parts of his body far removed from the source of the stimulation.

Hugh, by contrast, was most certainly dreaming. His muscles twitched occasionally; small, aborted movements muffled by his brain's production of glycine and gamma-aminobutyric acid during REM sleep.

Morpheus had been tracking the tiny movements of Hugh's body with half his attention. At first, he had not judged the dream to be an alarming one. Now, though, a small whine of distress escaped the human's lips. His breathing grew faster, and the arm around Morpheus tightened.

Before Morpheus could decide whether to roll over and wake Hugh from slumber, Hugh gave a full-body jerk and gasped into awareness. The human held his breath for a long moment as though assessing his surroundings for danger. Then he seemed to realize where he was, and with whom.

The tension drained from his muscles. He made a sleepy, wordless sound against the back of Morpheus' neck, tugging him closer until the gap between their hips closed. A hard length nudged the valley between his buttocks, rubbing firmly through two layers of thin clothing.

The trembling warmth that had been pooling in Morpheus' stomach coalesced into something sharper. Heavy heat filled his cock, which twitched and hardened.

The sensation was so novel that he froze, arrested.

As the God of Dreams, he had presided over eons of sexual interludes—usually as a detached overseer, but very occasionally as an active participant. In all cases, his involvement turned on the perceptions of the dreamer, not his own.

If the dreamer wished him to be awash in ecstasy and he chose to partake, that would be his experience of the dream. If the dreamer wished him cruel, then he was cruel. If they wished him tender, he was tender. Even during the singular occasion after Hugh had rescued him from the bunker and pleasured him in the waking world, it had been the worship that Morpheus desired, not the orgasm.

On that memorable occasion, Hugh's delight in the act of service had been so great, his own unfulfilled desire so sharp, that Morpheus had scaled heights of rapture previously unknown to his assumed physical form.

But this… was *different*.

He could not sense Hugh's dreams, nor his daydreams. Morpheus' physical awareness stopped short at the bounds of his all-too-mortal flesh. The surge of hungry heat originated *within him*. While it had doubtless been kindled by Hugh's warm proximity, it was not Hugh's desire.

It was his own.

Only when Hugh stilled behind him did Morpheus realize he'd gone rigid with shock, barely even breathing as he attempted to place this startling revelation into some sort of context.

"Sorry," Hugh rasped, his voice sleep-roughened. "Didn't mean to do that. I probably woke you up—" He shuffled backward on the mattress, putting a gap between them as his arm started to slide away.

Morpheus grabbed it and placed it around himself again, holding tight. "Don't stop," he said, striving for an imperial tone of command.

Now it was Hugh's turn to freeze.

"Oh," said his lover. After a slight hesitation, the human scooted close again, and Morpheus relaxed. The hand resting over his stomach slid lower, brushing over the front of the loose sleep pants he was wearing. "So… I take it you've discovered morning wood, then? And… you want to do something with it?"

Morpheus closed his eyes and arched into the touch, feeling sparks radiate outward from the light contact. "I wish for *you* to do something with it." He reversed course, pressing his hips back, and was rewarded with the rub of Hugh's hard stand again.

Hugh sucked in a sharp breath between his teeth. "Christ, you're a menace. Tell me if you don't like something."

Morpheus made a dismissive noise, which turned into a pleased hum as Hugh wrapped a hand around the jut of his hip and rutted against his arse with intent. The clothing separating them was an irritation, one that grew doubly irksome when he realized he couldn't simply wish it away. But before he could organize his limbs for the ungainly process of physically pushing the pajama bottoms over his hips and down his thighs without rising from the bed, Hugh's hand released his hip in favor of burrowing under the cotton shirt he was wearing.

Rough fingers found his left nipple with unerring accuracy, circling lightly until the flesh rose into a taut peak, then grasping and rolling the pebbled nub. Morpheus promptly forgot all about the pajama bottoms, his spine arching in pleasure.

"I dreamed about this," Hugh muttered, scraping a fingernail gently over the turgid point. "Dreamed about having you here in my bed, in the real world."

"The Night Lands are real," Morpheus protested.

Hugh's punishing pinch dragged a moan from him. "It's different, though. You know exactly what I mean—don't pretend that you don't."

"It *is* different, yes," Morpheus allowed. "For one thing, the process of dealing with clothing is far more vexing."

"Just needs a little teamwork, that's all," Hugh said, abandoning his nipple in favor of manhandling Morpheus onto his back. The human rose into a sitting position at his hips, grabbing the waistband of the offending loose pajama bottoms and giving a sharp tug. They surrendered to the onslaught, sliding over his hips and down his thighs, his cock springing free.

Hugh peeled them off his body like someone removing a glove, then urged Morpheus to sit up and slid the T-shirt over his head. Morpheus raised his arms helpfully, and a moment later, he was bare. He turned, grasping the waistband of Hugh's boxers—the only item of clothing he had worn to bed. With a bit of wriggling, Hugh, too, was naked.

"Better," Morpheus approved, raking fingertips through the coarse, dark hair adorning Hugh's chest.

"Much," Hugh agreed—catching the hand and lifting it to his lips before releasing it. "Now lie back, *leof*. I am going to make you feel *so good*. And this time, you won't be able to disappear on me immediately afterward."

Morpheus lay back as instructed, uncomfortably aware of how little he wished to disappear back

to his own realm, despite the many important reasons he needed to be there.

NINETEEN

SUCH RAW PHYSICALITY was not normally within Morpheus' experience. His was an existence made of dreamstuff—or it had been, until now. The last few days had been a sea of sensation, but much of it had consisted of discomfort, distress, and disgust.

He would never—*never*—have voluntarily sought existence as a mortal creature bound by flesh. The idea of being trapped permanently as such had barely entered his thoughts when he'd been scheming ways to retrieve Hugh's soul from his brothers' captivity. Had he known what would happen to him after the theft of the opal pendant, would he have gone through with his plan regardless?

He wasn't certain of the answer.

It was only now, only *here*, in Hugh's bed, that the siren lure of setting aside all his burdens hummed a melody of subtle seduction within the depths of his consciousness. Not, he thought wryly, that the sweet temptation of freedom from his inherent purpose overseeing the dreams of mortals was the *only* seduction currently taking place.

Hugh braced above him on bent arms, trailing open-mouthed kisses down the center of his chest.

"It always felt blasphemous somehow," he murmured into Morpheus' skin. "The idea of putting my mouth on you like this, I mean."

Morpheus gasped and arched as Hugh detoured to his right nipple, which was still tender and over-sensitized from the attention Hugh had paid it earlier. Morpheus clamped a hand around his nape to keep him there, unaware he'd even done so until Hugh's low moan of approval vibrated against his flesh.

"It *would* have been blasphemy," Morpheus said. "Though I doubt I'd have stopped you, even so."

"*Menace,*" Hugh repeated, punctuating the word with a sharp nip that startled a yelp from him.

"Hmm," he purred—whether in agreement, or merely approval as Hugh resumed his journey downward.

Halfway to his destination, the human paused. "Okay… I've gotta ask, though—because this has been driving me crazy. Why do you have a navel?"

Morpheus blinked down at him, his thoughts abruptly derailed. "Why would I *not* have a navel? Would the absence of one not appear strange?"

Hugh rested his chin in the offending divot and frowned thoughtfully. Morpheus' hand, still tangled in the fine hair at the base of his skull, twitched restlessly in response to the odd sensation of being touched there.

"I mean… it *would* seem odd, yes," Hugh said slowly. "But why would you *need* one? Or are gods born from the womb like humans?"

"Hugh," Morpheus began, "I have existed since long before humanity's ancestors first stood upright on two legs. And despite what some in the Night Lands might wish you to believe, humanity was *not* formed in our image." He huffed. "Rather the reverse, in fact."

Hugh appeared to chew on that for a long moment. "Huh. Why has that never occurred to me before, in eight hundred-plus years? Guess it wouldn't make sense that the Neanderthals were getting their dreams from a pale, skinny bloke with blue eyes."

Morpheus slid his hand free from Hugh's hair in favor of lounging back with his fingers laced behind his head, perfectly well aware of the picture he made.

"Perhaps because you seem rather enamored of this form," he suggested, affecting a bored tone. "It has made you biased."

Hugh chuckled. "You've got a god's ego, that's for sure. Impossible creature." His tone was fond. "I wonder if anyone's ever succeeded in fucking that cocksure attitude out of you before."

Morpheus opened his mouth to make some retort about smiting and the threat thereof, only to choke on the words when Hugh wrapped warm, faintly chapped lips around his stand, swirling his tongue around the sensitive head.

"You have my permission to attempt it," he managed hoarsely.

Hugh hummed agreement and sucked... a deep, drawing sensation that pulled from somewhere behind the navel that had so fascinated him a moment ago. Morpheus let his eyes slip closed to better focus on his internal perception.

His body's reaction was so... *intimate*. So *self-contained*. In the quiet room, its silence broken only by the wet sound of Hugh's mouth sliding up and down his shaft in an easy rhythm, nothing distracted from the thrum of heat and urgent desire spreading outward from the point of contact.

His thigh muscles trembled, an outward expression of the delicious push and pull of hot tension shifting inside him. It settled deeper, growing in urgency with every suck, every lick. Occasionally spiking when Hugh groaned and took him deeper, the tip of his cock sliding across the ridges of Hugh's hard palate.

Morpheus possessed only the human's occasional noises of pleasure, and the apparent enthusiasm of his movements, with which to judge his partner's enjoyment. The freedom of realizing that he was, in this moment, responsible only for his own pleasure, and not for a dreamer's, was briefly overwhelming.

His own desire.

It was such an alien concept that he struggled to place it in context—a process not helped by the urgent coil of heat ratcheting ever tighter in the pit of his belly. His mouth fell open. His balls drew up, drawn by the taut spring of pleasure growing ever more compressed inside him, straining to break free.

Hugh made another ravenous noise around his hard length, changing his angle and pressing down until his nose brushed Morpheus' pubic bone. Tight, enclosing heat squeezed the head of his cock, rippling convulsively as Hugh swallowed around the intrusion, gagging a little.

Without warning, the wonderful, terrible tension inside Morpheus broke like a dam collapsing under the strain of roaring floodwaters. Climax rocked him, his release pulsing and spilling down

Hugh's throat in strong spurts that wrung him dry, draining the strength from his body and the will from his mind.

And all the while, he had no sense of Hugh's subconscious — only the mouth on his cock and the hands grasping his hips.

His twitching muscles subsided into lax uselessness. A feeling of irrational belonging and wellbeing draped over his consciousness like a warm blanket, whispering that everything was perfect, and this was exactly where he was meant to be.

His stand softened inside Hugh's welcoming mouth, and Morpheus realized with distant fascination that he had no method for willing it to stay hard, should he have wished to do so. With a final, languid lick, Hugh let Morpheus' cock slip free, cool air replacing wet heat.

Morpheus made a low, satisfied sound, savoring the full-body hum of contentment for a moment longer before opening heavy eyelids to look down at Hugh's face.

"You are, as ever, a generous lover, my hunter," he said, his voice emerging as a leonine purr roughened by his earlier gasps and moans. "I wish to return the favor, but I can no longer sense your needs and desires directly. It is... *strange.*"

Hugh, still nestled between his legs, licked his lips. They were swollen and pink from heavy use, and his brown eyes watered, faintly reddened.

"First," he said, his voice even raspier than Morpheus' had been, "this isn't some kind of transaction, where you have to balance the ledger after every encounter."

Still buoyed by his body's release, Morpheus raised a teasing eyebrow. "Ah. So, you have no interest in reaching your own completion, then? Good to know."

Hugh sent a half-hearted glare up the length of his body. "Cheeky bastard. As it happens, I'm about ten seconds from rubbing myself off on the mattress like a teenager. But that doesn't have to be your problem if you don't want it to be."

Morpheus couldn't help a long-suffering sigh. "Don't be ridiculous. I am unsure where you gained this impression you seem to have, that I am some virginal ingenue who needs your protection from the coarse vulgarities of sex. You are my lover. I wish to see you well satisfied, by whatever means you desire—assuming it is still within my capability in this form."

Hugh seemed strangely overwhelmed by this, although Morpheus couldn't imagine why. He gaped for a moment before rallying, his expression falling into a comical pout. "Aw. So, no tentacles, then?"

It was Morpheus' turn to glare.

Hugh held the expression for an instant longer before it collapsed into a boyish grin. "Kidding. I'm *kidding*," he said. "And if you're game for it, I'd love to open you up and see if I can fuck another orgasm out of you. I've even got lube this time, because not having it on hand last time has been one of the great regrets of my ridiculously long life."

"I suppose that will be acceptable," Morpheus said, affecting a bored tone and marveling at the swell of lightness in his chest—one which threatened to erupt into a burble of outright laughter. With difficulty, he managed to stifle the impulse. Mortal or no, he still had an image to uphold, after all.

Hugh's grin turned wicked. He pushed off the bed, revealing an erection that did indeed appear to be in desperate need of attention. When he returned a moment later with a plastic bottle, however, he dove into the task of easing Morpheus open with a single-minded focus and determination that soon had him writhing and mindless once more.

Morpheus rode the waves of this new assault on his mortal body's nervous system, enjoying the ways it was similar and different to what had come before. When Hugh finally sank into him, filling him in a way fingers never could, they scaled the peak together. Morpheus clenched, fresh spend splattering between them as Hugh groaned and spilled into him, pumping Morpheus' cock with firm strokes all the while.

Afterward, Morpheus gave only a token protest as Hugh rose and returned with warm, damp wash towels to clean him up. They lay together for some time, languid and louche, tangled together in the golden light of morning.

Morpheus, who had been idly watching the quality of the light change through the room's small window, stretched.

"I find myself curious about your life beyond this cottage," he said. "Perhaps I might accompany you when you next venture abroad. It is odd to think of it, but beyond our centenary meetings—and my unfortunate capture in 1940 — I have spent very little time in the Sublunary."

Hugh's hand paused in its rhythmic stroking up and down Morpheus' shoulder and bicep. His entire body went still. Curious, Morpheus rolled over to look at him.

The human's face was a blank mask. "Erm," he said. "Yes. About that…"

TWENTY

THE FLUTTERING THRUM of panic so soon after a shattering orgasm made Hugh's head spin unpleasantly. And yet, Morpheus' request to see more of the waking world shouldn't have come as a surprise.

It *wasn't* a surprise—not really. He'd just thought he'd have more time to figure out the best response, that was all.

"Erm," he said. "Yes. About that…"

If Morpheus saw firsthand the insanity and rampant paranoia that had people setting fire to stores and threatening to overload nuclear reactors, he would immediately insist on trying to confront Phobetor. Hugh wasn't sure Morpheus would be able to *find* Phobetor, now that he was stuck as a mortal… but he also wasn't sure he *wouldn't*.

And Morpheus was far too weak right now to battle a god. For fuck's sake, he'd been draped over a toilet puking his guts out mere days ago. He barely ate half as much food as Hugh wanted him to, and he was so skinny that he looked like a strong gust of wind could knock him flat on his arse.

The world had slowly been going to hell in a handbasket for years now. For *decades*. It could wait another few weeks while Morpheus regained his strength, and they managed to come up with some sort of workable plan to get his godhood back. Hugh's decision had nothing whatsoever to do with Morpheus' presence in his bed.

In his arms.

He cleared his throat, certain now of what he needed to do.

"I've, uh, been meaning to check in with a client of mine," he continued. "I can't remember now if I told you this, but I've been working as a farrier again, these last few years."

"I was aware," Morpheus said, with a languid, self-satisfied little smile that had Hugh's cock contemplating a second round. "There is a pleasing symmetry to it, is there not? You were a farrier when first we met."

"Yeah," Hugh agreed. "It's... comforting, I guess? To know how to do something that was valuable in the thirteenth century, and have the knowledge still be valuable today. Anyway, I'll be seeing this client soon. You could come with me?"

Mary Walthorpe had called him two days ago, informing him that Steph—the young farrier he'd handed most of his clients to—had returned to Leatherhead to look after her mother. Apparently, the woman had been seriously injured in a random knife attack on a bus. Hugh had been intending to track down a different farrier to shoe Mary's horses, but he could as easily do them himself.

Two birds with one stone, and all that. He could take Morpheus somewhere pleasant and peaceful, while also scrubbing away the horrific image Phobetor had implanted in his brain—Morpheus torturing Mary and her family to madness, not even sparing the animals from his revenge against Hugh.

Even as Phobetor's creatures had been tormenting him, Hugh had known there was something deeply and unutterably wrong with the scene playing out inside his head... but nevertheless, the image remained. He would confront it once and for all with the truth, exorcizing it from his mind.

"That would be agreeable," Morpheus said, and Hugh made a mental note to call Mary first thing after breakfast.

———◆———

The weather was far more pleasant than it had been the last time Hugh pulled into the Walthorpes' stable yard. It was chilly enough at night that Hugh was extremely glad to have fixed his front door, but at this time of year, the days were warm when the sun was out.

Iridaceae had declined Hugh's offer to join them with rolled eyes and an attitude of utter disinterest.

"Why would I want to go someplace where I'd have to interact with *people*?" she'd asked, curling her lip in distaste. Baphometh had punctuated the question with a disdainful meow, so Hugh and Morpheus had left them to it.

In addition to the basic clothing Hugh had purchased for Morpheus during his fateful trip to Sandhurst, he'd ordered a wider selection of items online and had them delivered. As much as he'd been avoiding the internet and all its associated madness until quite recently, he'd grown to understand its appeal.

Barring occasional gaps in the global supply chain, a person could get almost anything they could imagine shipped to their house within days, even in the face of pandemics, madness, and domestic terrorism.

Morpheus was wearing black wellies, black denim jeans, and a knitted sweater in a soft dove gray pattern that brought out his eyes. Hugh had also laid in a fresh supply of masks, after explaining their necessity and proper usage to both his guests.

The current virus was no threat to him personally — no more than any of the other plagues that had come and gone over the centuries. But for all they knew, Morpheus and Iridaceae might be as vulnerable as any other humans. And Hugh would cut off his right arm rather than risk bringing illness to his elderly client and her family.

"Hello, my dear," Mary greeted warmly as he stepped out of the van. She, by contrast, was unmasked, her round, wrinkled face creased in a smile. "So good to see you — and to be seen!"

"Hey! Did you get the vaccine?" Hugh asked. "That's wonderful!"

"It's been two weeks and three days since my second dose," she said. "No more mask lines or fogged-up spectacles!"

Morpheus closed the van door and joined them, stretching after sharing the passenger seat with a selection of tools that wouldn't fit in the back.

"Good afternoon," he greeted formally.

"Sorry," Hugh said. "Should've done introductions right up front. Mary, this is a friend of mine who's been staying with me. He wanted to get out of the house for a bit, and I thought, where better? Morpheus, Mary Walthorpe. Mary, this is Morpheus."

Mary raised her eyebrows, but she stuck out a hand gamely. "What a terribly classical name! It's a pleasure to meet you. Any friend of Hugh's..."

Morpheus took the offered hand for a delicate shake. "The pleasure is mine, madam. Your property is quite impressive. A dream for many, I feel certain."

Hugh shot him a look. He'd decided, after some deliberation, not to make any awkward attempts at an alias. Morpheus was an unusual name, to put it mildly. However, he'd figured it was better to brazen it out than risk calling him Morty or Marvin only to slip up later. But if the man was going to stand around making quips about dreams...

"For us, this is simply what our family has always done," Mary said, evidently not finding anything amiss with the remark. "Come into the barn, both of you. George should have the first horse ready and waiting for you, Hugh. He threw a shoe last week and has a nasty quarter-crack in the right fore. Hence my urgent need for a farrier."

Hugh strapped on his leather apron and grabbed a hoof stand, following her into the stable as Morpheus tagged along behind. As promised, George was waiting with a huge, raw-boned gelding. It was the same horse that had been down in his stall in the throes of a poisoned dream the last time Hugh had been here.

"What a magnificent creature," Morpheus said. "With such a long hip and sloping shoulder, he must have immense scope over jumps."

Mary perked up, and George eyed Morpheus with interest over his mask.

"You've got a fine eye for hunters, it seems," Mary said.

Hugh picked up the gelding's right foreleg and applied himself to inspecting the crack, resolutely trying not to blush like a schoolgirl at the unintentional double entendre.

A fine eye for hunters, indeed.

Behind him, Mary and Morpheus fell into a discussion of horseflesh—because apparently horses featured heavily in dreams, or else were a particular interest of Greek gods.

Possibly both.

By the time Hugh had cleaned out the crack, applied a corrective shoe, and patched the gap with epoxy, Mary had extended an invitation for Morpheus to come back and try out a young mare she was particularly proud of. Hugh listened to the entire exchange with something like shock, trying to decide how offended he should be that it had taken him a full five hundred years to get as many words out of Morpheus as Mary had managed in the last forty-five minutes.

The afternoon passed pleasantly enough, Hugh falling into the familiar rhythms of the work. He kept half an ear on his client and his lover as Mary gave Morpheus the full guided tour, even disappearing to the kennels for a bit. Gradually, reality nudged out the lingering traces of Phobetor's cruel hallucinations.

He'd begun to relax, just finishing up with the final horse when the pair returned. "There we go," Hugh told George, straightening up. "All done."

"Thank you for coming out on such short notice," Mary said. "And for bringing such a charming companion with you. It's so refreshing to meet someone else who's managed to escape the madness."

Abruptly, Hugh's brief foray into relaxation snapped back into tension. He laughed awkwardly. "Yes, well, the cities have always been a bit mad. Much better to stay out here in the country."

He wasn't sure if he was imagining Morpheus' gaze on him—but Mary paid him and they parted cheerfully enough, with a repetition of her invitation for both of them to come out sometime soon for a hack.

The drive back to the cottage was quiet. Morpheus seemed to be in a pensive mood, while Hugh was in more of a mild panic. What had Mary told him, exactly?

Morpheus didn't raise the subject, however, so Hugh tried to let it go. He parked the van, grabbed the tools that would need to be sharpened, and then excused himself for a shower before dinner, leaving Morpheus and Iridaceae alone in the living room.

When he emerged twenty minutes later, it was to the jarring scene of Morpheus hunched over Hugh's laptop with Iridaceae leaning over his shoulder, pointing at something on the keyboard.

"Um," Hugh said, his nagging sense of panic from earlier swelling.

Morpheus looked up, pinning him with mild blue eyes. "Iridaceae has just been introducing me to the *world wide web*. From the news sites, it appears my brother has been increasingly active in the human realm. Out of curiosity, were you intending to inform me of this fact at some point?"

TWENTY-ONE

CLAMMY SWEAT BROKE out on Hugh's palms as images of Morpheus fighting Phobetor — of Morpheus captured, or tortured, or driven mad with fear, or lying dead on the ground — crowded into his head.

His vision swam, going gray and tunnel-like. He grabbed the edge of the wall, swaying in the room's open doorway as he tried and failed to find words. His lungs seized, refusing to inflate and draw in air.

It was a sensation he recognized from the years after the First World War. A part of his mind whispered that this reaction was not proportionate with the situation, while a different part screamed that *yes*, it bloody well *was*! Morpheus was going to leave, he was going to put himself in danger of losing his mortal *life*, and Hugh would be *alone* —

The object of Hugh's icy dread frowned; the desk chair scraping backward as he rose quickly and hurried across the room. His angular features loomed at the center of Hugh's tunneling vision. Cool hands that had never known physical labor cupped Hugh's cheeks, the skin silky smooth against his stubble.

Somehow, Hugh was sliding down the wall in a barely controlled collapse — Morpheus following him down with alarm flaring in his brilliant blue gaze. Again, the internal voice whispered that this reaction wasn't normal... that he must look ridiculous.

"Breathe," Morpheus said, and Hugh tried to focus on the little wrinkle of concern forming between those dark, finely drawn brows.

He could either breathe, or not. It wasn't as though a lack of oxygen would kill him permanently. But his lungs eventually made the decision for him, expanding far enough to draw in a wheezing breath, and another, and another.

"Is he all right?" Iridaceae's uncertain tone filtered through the pounding in his ears.

"No," Morpheus said. "I do not believe he is."

Hugh tried to focus on the cool points of contact cradling his face, slapping numb hands over Morpheus' fingers to keep them there.

"Please don't try to fight him," he begged in a raspy whisper. "Please, Morpheus—he'll *kill* you..."

"Iridaceae," Morpheus murmured, "it might be best if you gave us some privacy."

"No argument here," Iridaceae said, sidling past Hugh's slumped body in the doorway as though she was worried that sudden-onset hysteria might be contagious. "Try to fix him, okay? I don't like him like this."

Morpheus waited a few seconds until she'd gone, then turned his full attention back to Hugh.

Hugh licked his lips, the gray fog receding a tiny bit. "I had to keep you from finding out how bad things are. I had to keep you safe."

Panic threatened again at the reminder that he'd *failed*, that Morpheus *knew*.

A smooth thumb stroked the sensitive skin under Hugh's left eye. He could feel moisture smearing beneath the touch. Was he weeping?

"You feared what would happen when I discovered the extent of the damage my brother has done," Morpheus said.

"Of course I did! You can't take him on," Hugh babbled. "Morpheus, you mustn't!"

No," Morpheus said. "Stop. Listen to my words. You *feared* what would happen."

Hugh's jaw snapped shut. "Wh-what?" he whispered.

"I have watched you face down a crazed woman pointing a gun at you, my hunter," Morpheus said. "I have seen you beg for mercy on behalf of your own torturers. And now, for *this*, you tremble with fear? What do you think I can do with this information, mortal as I currently am? My brother may not even be in this realm."

A shred of rationality threaded its way through Hugh's raw terror. He licked his lips, the sense of Morpheus' words gradually penetrating.

"Phobetor? This feeling is *Phobetor's* doing?" he asked, mortification flooding in to replace the fear.

The hands cupping his cheeks slid away. Morpheus sat back on his heels, letting his forearms rest loosely over his knees.

"The embodiment of fear is wreaking havoc on the human realm. You may be immortal, Hugh de Ferrers—but immortality does not make you immune to the power of gods."

Hugh made a valiant effort to reorder his thoughts around this new and completely unwelcome revelation. Aside from that awful stretch of time he'd spent trapped in Hallucination, he'd believed himself an oasis of normality—Phobetor's curse of fear and paranoia somehow circling around him without touching him. *Other people* were acting crazy… not *him*.

"Oh, fucking *hell*," he cursed. "Fucking… *fuck*." Anger joined the swirl of mortification and stale terror. "God *damnit!*"

"Unfortunately, I do not currently possess the capacity," Morpheus said dryly. "And even in less trying times, damnation is more my uncle's domain than mine."

Hugh thought of the grimly intimidating figure of Death and found that he wasn't terribly surprised by that. He grasped Morpheus' slender shoulders, aware that his hands were shaking. "You promise you won't run off?"

Morpheus lifted his eyebrows. "Run off where?" he asked tartly. "And to do what? We are in an isolated cottage hidden away deep in the woods."

But Hugh only squeezed tighter, his fingertips digging into flesh.

With a sigh, Morpheus held his gaze and said, "Yes, I promise that I will not take rash action."

The last of the irrational fear drained away. Not *gone*, exactly… but receding into the unseen psychological swamp where it usually lurked.

I'm sorry," Hugh said hoarsely. "I should have told you what was happening sooner."

Morpheus made a noncommittal humming noise. "The knowledge would not have been a benefit during those first difficult days after my godhood was stolen. And you are a victim of my brother's cruelty as much as any other creature in the Sublunary. More than most, in fact."

"He showed me visions of you torturing Mary Walthorpe and her family to punish me for defying you." The confession poured out in a rush, as though once his secrets had started unraveling, he was compelled to spill all of them. "Their animals, too. The dogs and horses. You sent them all mad."

Morpheus closed his eyes, his head dipping. A faint tremor rippled through the lithe body beneath Hugh's grip.

"Even while it was happening, I knew that it couldn't be right," he hurried to add. "I knew it had to be some kind of a trick, or…"

He trailed off as Morpheus' eyes opened again, realizing that the former god was shaking with *rage*, not sadness.

"When you were captured and beaten, I punished your torturers in defiance of your wishes," Morpheus said softly. "But I do not punish innocents."

It was Hugh's turn to lift a hand to the other man's cheek. "No. I get that now. I *do*."

Morpheus turned his face into the touch for a brief moment, pressing against the contact like a cat. Hugh got the impression he was mastering himself. When he straightened away, the rage was gone from behind his eyes… or at least buried.

"Come," Morpheus said. "I would know more details of what has been happening in the mortal realm. The news sites offer only a biased and fragmented view."

Hugh accepted a hand up, rising onto rubbery legs. "About that," he said, striving for a lighter tone and falling short. "I'm still trying to wrap my brain around the God of Nightmares using the internet."

"It is a truly fascinating invention." Morpheus tilted his head. "I can see the logical progression from the telegraph and television, though in truth, it resembles nothing which has come before. Also, its use is not terribly intuitive, to put it mildly."

"Forget that part. How did you even get past the password on the laptop?" Hugh asked, bewildered.

Morpheus quirked an eyebrow. "I'm reliably informed that you allowed a sentient owl to perch on your shoulder while doing research and reading email on the same machine."

Hugh resisted the urge to slap a hand over his face. "That feathered little traitor," he muttered.

"I believe you'll find that her loyalty to me predates her loyalty to you," Morpheus said, sounding mildly amused. Then, he sobered. "You have extracted my word that I will not act rashly. However, you must already know that the situation in the Sublunary cannot be allowed to continue unchecked."

The fear bubbled up again, but Hugh quashed it. Knowing it didn't originate solely within his own psyche helped.

"I understand that," he said. "But I'm damned if I know how to proceed. Do you have any idea what Phobetor's endgame is? I mean… does he want humanity to destroy the world with a global thermonuclear war? Or would that cut off his food source?"

"Food source?" Morpheus echoed blankly. He shook his head. "No, I believe you misunderstand the nature of my brother's powers. The only goal of the God of Fear is to make living creatures afraid. What happens as a consequence of that fear is of limited interest to him."

Hugh blinked. "Okay, that's actually terrifying." He paused. "Which is bitterly ironic, I suppose. It's just that… humans are awfully good at destroying things when they're afraid."

"I am aware," Morpheus said, dry as bone dust. He sighed. "I must consider the options, such as they are. There is one possibility…" He trailed off.

"Yes?" Hugh asked.

But Morpheus shook his head, repeating, "I must consider things. But for now, perhaps we should return to preparations for a meal before discussing the details. Doubtless Iridaceae will be relieved to find your equanimity restored."

After even such a small evasion, Hugh wasn't certain *equanimity* was the correct adjective to describe his current mental state. But the knowledge that his emotions weren't necessarily his own allowed him to crush the little burst of adrenaline that spiked his pulse.

He had Morpheus' word that he wouldn't run off and throw himself into danger. For now, that had to be enough.

TWENTY-TWO

MORPHEUS HAD KNOWN, on some level, that any daydreams of renouncing his responsibilities in favor of lounging in an idyllic cottage with his human lover were just that. Daydreams. He, of all beings, should recognize them well enough.

He was unprepared for the sinking sensation he'd experienced in his rebellious mortal stomach upon discovering the true state of the Sublunary. Perhaps he would not have pursued the issue, had it not been for Mary Walthorpe's casual words about escaping the madness—and Hugh's reaction of alarm upon overhearing them.

There had been other clues, of course. The horses at the Walthorpes' farm had been nervous and fretful, despite the care and competence of their handlers. The dogs had whined piteously in their roomy kennels, despite Mary's crooned words of reassurance.

"Things seemed to be getting better for a while," the old woman had said sadly. "It doesn't matter so much for me, but I hate to think of the younger generations trapped in such a world."

"Perhaps we can all dream of better times to come," had been all he could think of to say, still unsure as he was of the situation in the wider world.

Mary Walthorpe had squeezed his arm in agreement or reassurance, and though it should indeed have been blasphemous for a mortal to touch him in such a familiar manner without his express permission, he found that he did not mind the gesture.

Then there was Hugh himself. Morpheus had failed in his duty of care toward the human. He'd been cognizant of the trauma Hugh must have gone through at his brothers' hands. Yet, he'd taken Hugh at his word that he did not wish to speak about it.

Perhaps that had been the truth; in fact, it probably was. But it was obvious, looking back, that Phobetor would have used Morpheus as a weapon with which to wound Hugh.

No matter his own woes, Morpheus should have done better. Hearing the content of the visions his brother had used to torment his lover made his thoughts turn to violence against his own blood-kin. He wished to visit upon Phobetor the same pain he had caused Hugh, multiplied a thousandfold.

As for Phantasos, the depth of betrayal Morpheus felt was shocking. He and his younger brother had done little but snipe at each other for millennia… but once upon a time, they had been close, just as their realms were.

What had *happened* to them all?

Once, the Night Lands had existed in, if not harmony, then at least tranquility. Now, Morpheus found himself sorely tempted to give Phobetor the war he so clearly wanted.

A foolish notion indeed, given that he was currently trapped in a mortal body after having been severely weakened by Phobetor's *last* gambit against him.

And that was the crux of the issue, was it not? Phobetor *could not* be allowed to continue his rampage through the mortal realm. Yet Morpheus, the only one of his family who apparently gave a damn about the injustice of what was happening in the Sublunary, was powerless to stop him.

He had pulled back from exposing the final playing card in his hand to Hugh. Whether that had been an act of strategy or one of cowardice was open to interpretation. On the one hand, Morpheus did not think Hugh had been in an emotional state to accept the information with anything approaching equanimity. On the other hand, while his promise not to 'run off,' as Hugh had put it, might be technically accurate... offering it without also explaining what he might have to do instead had been facile at best.

They were together in Hugh's bed. Morpheus sat with his back resting against the headboard, deep in thought. The human was sleeping now, thankfully — curled up against Morpheus' hip. One arm rested across the blankets covering his thighs as though desperate to ensure Morpheus didn't slip away during the night.

Hugh had been exhausted after their discussion earlier, as well he might be. The weight of his well-meaning deception — not to mention the stress of the last few weeks — had caught up with him all at once, it seemed.

Meanwhile, Morpheus found his mind unwilling to slow. The need to *act* made him twitchy with impatience... but the situation was not that simple.

His dark thoughts were interrupted by the soft rustle of someone moving around in the kitchen. An unwelcome surge of adrenaline activated receptors in his sympathetic nervous system, increasing his respiration and heartrate. It was irrational. No sounds of doors or windows being forced open had preceded the quiet noises inside the cottage.

It was obviously Iridaceae helping herself to Hugh's food. She was a nocturnal creature by nature, just as he himself was.

Succumbing to the need for conversation, Morpheus assessed his odds of getting out of bed without waking his companion. They were low to nonexistent. And, even if they hadn't been, Morpheus was aware of how it might affect Hugh to wake in the night and find himself unexpectedly alone.

The necessity of accounting for another person's emotions when making simple decisions was novel. Nevertheless, it was a small concession in the face of all the human had done for him. It was also, he suspected, the very lowest of bars when it came to being a good lover.

As little as he liked the thought of disturbing Hugh's much-needed rest, he closed a hand on the human's shoulder, shaking it lightly until Hugh groaned and blinked awake.

"Wha...?" Hugh asked. "What is it, what's wrong?"

"All is well," Morpheus assured him, turning his light grip into a caress. "Iridaceae is awake, and she seems restless. I'm going to the kitchen to speak with her. I didn't want you to wake while I was gone and worry."

"Oh." Hugh settled back in the nest of covers, already half-asleep again. "S'good. Thanks for that, *leof*. Lemme know if…"

The words descended into mumbled nonsense, and then to light snoring. Confident that Hugh would not wake again for some time, Morpheus gently untangled himself from the covers and the restraining arm, which clutched tighter for a moment before releasing him.

Barefoot, clad in a long-sleeved shirt and the soft pajama bottoms Hugh had purchased for him, Morpheus padded down the hallway to the kitchen. It was mercifully free of burglars.

The overhead lights were off, but the light inside the refrigerator unit silhouetted Iridaceae's slight form as she rummaged through its contents.

"Oh, hello," she said, without looking around or pausing in her search. "Do you want some leftover curry?"

"No, thank you," he told her politely, all too aware of the potential effects of late-night leftover curry on the dreaming mind. So far, he was not aware of having any dreams as a newly minted mortal. However, some of his oneiri harbored enough resentment toward him that he did not wish to tempt fate.

She shrugged her indifference and emerged with a white takeout carton. Morpheus crossed to the stove and turned on the small light in the hood above it, offering them a bit of illumination as Iridaceae closed the refrigerator door.

She perched on one of the kitchen chairs, peering at him curiously. "Couldn't sleep?"

"I have been thinking," he said.

"About the humans going crazy and hurting each other?" She poked a fork into the container and shoveled yellow rice into her mouth, still watching him.

"Yes," he replied. "I cannot allow the situation to continue."

She swallowed, her fork pausing on its return trip to the carton. "Do you have a choice?" Her graceful brows drew together. "I mean… no offense, but you're stuck in a human body, and even if you knew how to drive, you can't exactly chase down a god using Hugh's van."

"It is true I will need assistance," he allowed.

She set the fork down on the table. "What kind of assistance?"

"My uncle's," Morpheus said, quashing the all-too-human sense of dread that came with the admission.

Iridaceae settled back in her chair, her frown deepening. "Thanatus won't help. I tried! All he did was throw me out of his realm. Unless you don't believe me—"

Hurt had crept into her expression.

"No," he said quickly. "I am aware of your efforts on my behalf, and I thank you for them, Iridaceae." Her hurt look subsided, shifting back to wariness as he continued. "Unfortunately, you lacked the leverage necessary to move Thanatus to action."

"What's that supposed to mean?" she demanded, crossing her arms tightly.

"*You* did not win a bet against him in 1421 A.D., where the stakes were an unspecified favor to be redeemed at a future date."

She gaped at him, her jaw hanging open until she noticed and closed her mouth with an audible click of teeth. She blinked at him.

"You *what*, now?" she asked, incredulous.

Morpheus sighed. "The wager over Hugh. That was the prize I won from my uncle."

"I thought you wagered control of some land within your realms!" she said.

"That was what he asked for, as his side of the stakes," Morpheus replied, as patiently as he could. "I hoped to discourage him by asking for a far more valuable boon. I demanded a future favor, assuming he would become angry at my presumption and call the whole thing off."

"He didn't, obviously." Her tone was flat.

"He did not," Morpheus agreed, aware that he had gained something much more valuable than a simple favor from one of the gods in the process. He had gained Hugh's regard.

Unfortunately, he might end up losing the latter by collecting on the former.

"But..." Uncertainty twisted his familiar's pixie-like features. "Thanatus is in the Night Lands, and you are trapped here, in the Sublunary."

"Yes."

"So how can you reach him to demand payment on the wager?" she asked.

"That," Morpheus said heavily, "is rather the problem."

TWENTY-THREE

IRIDACEAE ROSE ABRUPTLY to her feet, chair legs scraping across tile with an unpleasant screech.

"You're going to do something stupid," she said.

Morpheus sighed. "Iridaceae—"

"No!" his familiar said sharply. "Stay there. Don't move!"

She disappeared into the depths of the cottage. Morpheus contemplated the optics of staying where he was, versus running after her. He stayed, although he did relinquish his post by the stove in favor of pacing back and forth across the small room. He could guess where she'd gone, and his suspicions were confirmed when she returned a minute later towing a groggy Hugh behind her.

"Tell him he's being stupid," she demanded, shoving the human to stand in front of Morpheus, blocking his path.

Hugh blinked at him in a manner that seemed ironically rather owlish.

"What?" he said plaintively. "What are you talking about? Why is he being stupid?"

"Because he wants to make good on the wager he won against Thanatus, and there's only one way for a mortal to meet the God of Death!" Iridaceae snapped.

Hugh continued to look back and forth between them with the air of someone who'd just been awakened from a sound sleep for the second time in one night. The silence stretched painfully, until Morpheus wished for a knife to cut through the tension.

"Right," Hugh said eventually. "It's three in the morning, and this sounds like a conversation that's going to require coffee."

"I want tea," Iridaceae said.

"Coffee and tea," Hugh agreed, and shuffled over to put the kettle on.

Once Hugh and Iridaceae were seated at the table with their beverages of choice, Morpheus reluctantly sat down as well.

"Talk," Hugh said.

"You are aware that my uncle and I made a wager about your willingness to embrace immortality," Morpheus began, knowing that the subject was a sensitive one.

Hugh swallowed a sip of the scalding liquid in his mug and set it down. "Yes..." he said cautiously.

"I don't believe I ever shared the stakes with you," Morpheus continued.

"No," Hugh said, still in that wary tone. "I don't believe you did." He paused, as though gathering himself. "So, go on then. What do gods offer up as an ante?"

"You must understand, it was Thanatus who proposed the wager in the first place," Morpheus said. "He suggested I pledge a portion of my realm in the Night Lands. I had no interest in his proposal, and I thought to dissuade him from the venture by demanding something more valuable than he would be willing to gamble."

Hugh's heavy brows furrowed. "What sort of something?"

"An undefined future favor."

The human's brown eyes bore into his, intense. "I don't think I understand. Why would you believe that would put him off? He's your *uncle*. Wouldn't he offer you a favor if you asked for one, simply because you're his nephew?"

Iridaceae made a strange, choked noise and suddenly grew very interested in the contents of her teacup.

Morpheus raised an eyebrow. "You have *met* my family, have you not?"

Hugh continued to stare at him for a long moment before his expression smoothed over.

"Okay, fair point. Your relatives are arseholes." He took a larger swig from his mug, as though it contained much-needed brandy rather than coffee. "So, Thanatus agreed to the stakes, and he lost because I'm a stubborn sod who wasn't ready to die. Meaning you have a favor due, and you want to collect. That was the 'possibility' you mentioned yesterday but didn't want to talk about."

"Yes," Morpheus admitted.

"Only you're mortal now," Hugh went on. "You can't just put the God of Death on speed-dial and say you need the favor he owes you. And Iridaceae says you're about to do something stupid... because there's only one way for a mortal to get a face-to-face meeting with your uncle." He tapped his fingertips rhythmically on the tabletop. "Sounds like she's right about the stupid part."

Morpheus scowled.

"Tell me this, though," Hugh said. "Just because someone owes you a favor, it doesn't necessarily mean they can follow through with what you want. If you're able to collect this favor from Thanatus, does he have the wherewithal to get your godhood back? Can he stop Phobetor?"

"My uncle is the most powerful god of his generation," Morpheus said. "Only my grandparents, Kronos and Chaos, wield more influence over creation."

"Chaos and… time? Your grandparents are *chaos and time*?" Hugh paused, pinching the bridge of his nose and worrying the skin between his eyes. "No, right, of course they are. *Fuck.*" He looked up, his hand falling limp to the table. "So… I guess that's a yes, then?"

"Yes," Morpheus confirmed. "I should have pursued this avenue the moment I realized that Phobetor had stolen the opal pendant, but—"

"No, you shouldn't have," Hugh interrupted. "Because Iridaceae's right, and you're being incredibly dense about this."

Morpheus opened his mouth to object, but Hugh waved him down.

"Stop and think, *leof.* You're sleeping with a bloke who *doesn't stay dead.*" Hugh straightened in the chair, squaring his shoulders. "You need someone to give the Grim Reaper a message? I'm your man. I'll even promise not to spit on him this time."

"I don't think that will work," Iridaceae said uncertainly. "I already asked Thanatus for help on Morpheus' behalf. He laughed in my face and kicked me out of his realm."

But a glint of stubbornness had crept into Hugh's gaze. "You didn't know about the favor, though. Not until just now—that's why you woke me up. So, you couldn't have invoked it, am I right?"

"Well, no..." Iridaceae replied. "That's true, I suppose."

"There you go." Hugh gestured vaguely. "I just have to make it clear that Morpheus wants to collect what Death owes him. Who better to deliver the message? I was the focus of the bet, after all."

He would also be an unwelcome reminder of Thanatus' humiliating defeat, Morpheus knew. Not that such a thing would cause a god to renege on his word—but that was not the only problem.

"Iridaceae is correct," Morpheus said. "I do not believe your proposal will succeed."

"Why wouldn't it?" Hugh demanded, his tone growing truculent. "You know as well as anyone how many times I've died. You were *there* for some of them."

"And have you ever encountered my uncle during your forays beyond the veil?" Morpheus asked pointedly.

Hugh's righteous conviction wavered. Morpheus watched as he gathered it around himself again like a cloak.

"I could have done," he said. "Maybe I just don't remember it afterward."

"And will your untethered soul *remember* to pass on a detailed message to a creature far beyond your ken, while trapped in the throes of death?" Morpheus pressed.

Hugh's temper flared. "If it keeps you from doing something idiotic, you're damn right I will!"

Morpheus found his human heart thudding too fast and too loudly; his palms sweating in his lap. This physical reaction to emotion was another aspect of mortality he found nigh-on intolerable.

"What can it hurt to try?" Iridaceae said, acting as the unlikely voice of reason.

What if Thanatus grew angry, Morpheus thought, and decided to rescind his promise not to reap Hugh's soul? What if the human did not revive? What if Morpheus' foolish overconfidence resulted in the destruction of the one creature in all of reality who cherished Morpheus for *who* he was, rather than *what* he was?

Stop, Morpheus told himself. *Enough. You are being irrational.*

Thanatus would not go back on his word. Not about Hugh's immortality, and not about the debt he owed from the wager.

"I do not wish you to do this," he said, startled by how hoarse his voice sounded. He cleared his throat.

"None of us is *happy* about it, you fool," Hugh replied.

"You should let him try it," Iridaceae said. She turned her attention to Hugh. "What's the best way? Can we do it now?"

Hugh looked taken aback. Then he lifted his coffee to his lips and muttered something about *bloodthirsty feathered menaces*. He drained the rest of the mug and set it down with a clink.

"Let me have a piss and a wash first. Christ, I'm going to need something a lot stronger than coffee for this." He scrubbed both hands roughly over his face. "Okay. Okay, let me think. Something that won't make a mess, and preferably something that won't take forever to repair itself afterward. I can… um… drink a bottle of vodka, and one of you can shove a pillow over my face after I pass out."

"That sounds simple," Iridaceae said cheerfully. "I'll do it."

Hugh eyed her narrowly. "You know, it's a good thing I like you," he said, "Because you're fucking terrifying sometimes."

Morpheus sat rigid, battling unwanted and unhelpful somatic reactions over the prospect of watching Hugh die on his behalf. Hugh's attention fell on him a moment later, and his gaze softened.

"Don't look like that," he said. "You'd do the same thing for me. In fact, you were going to."

The words *because you're an idiot* hung in the air, unspoken.

"I do not deserve you," Morpheus said quietly past the obstruction in his throat—a physical manifestation, he suspected, of his foolish pride.

"Eh, maybe not," Hugh said. "Seems like you're kind of stuck with me, though."

In the background, Iridaceae looked between them and did an exaggerated impression of someone gagging in disgust.

186

TWENTY-FOUR

GETTING BLACKOUT DRUNK wasn't nearly as fun as it sounded, but at least Hugh was in a period of his life where his alcohol tolerance was relatively low. There had been stretches where actually getting drunk enough to pass out would have been an expensive and time-consuming proposition.

Since all he had on hand was a half-finished bottle of wine and another of cooking sherry, their morbid experiment had to wait until the off-license shop in the village opened for business at eight. Normally, Hugh would have bicycled down and back rather than driving the van, but to be brutally honest, he didn't think having an extended period of time for quiet contemplation would do him any favors on this day.

That, and he wasn't one hundred percent confident that leaving Morpheus alone for so long would be safe. There was a small but non-zero chance that, given an opportunity, he'd do something stupid in a foolish attempt at saving Hugh from what Morpheus apparently saw as an act of self-sacrifice.

Hugh wasn't sure why Morpheus seemed so hung up about it. While he wasn't one to seek out transient oblivion for jollies, the worst self-sacrifice this was likely to entail was giving himself a truly vile hangover.

Aside from the resulting headache, the only part that gave him pause was the prospect of seeing Thanatus in person again. It had been... what? Six centuries since he'd crossed paths with the God of

Death? And that brief meeting had not, as they say, gone well.

In Hugh's mind, this was mostly down to Thanatus being an arsehole. Based on Iridaceae's description of trying to seek his help after her run-in with Phobetor, it didn't sound like much had changed since the fifteenth century.

But a wager was a wager, and all Hugh had to do was deliver a simple message—Morpheus was ready to collect his debt. Even while dead, how hard could it be?

Trusting that Iridaceae would prevent Morpheus from doing something stupid during Hugh's brief trip to acquire vodka, Hugh coaxed the aging van into life and drove along winding roads with the morning sun struggling weakly through a covering of high, thin clouds.

As he approached the familiar outskirts of the sleepy village, a pair of panda cars whizzed past him, lights and sirens flashing. He steadied his nerves and continued on, resolutely driving past an impressive collection of law enforcement and fire service vehicles congregated around the old sixteenth century parish church set back from the village crossroads.

The off-license wasn't really a *proper* off-license. More accurately, it was a tiny shop crammed into the corner of a slightly larger shop that sold pantry staples and other household sundries. Still, it had a precarious-looking shelf stuffed with liquor bottles along the back wall, next to a small, glass fronted cooler stuffed equally full of beer cans.

Hugh chose the cheaper of the two bottles of vodka on display and took it to the till. The gruff, balding man hunched on a stool behind the counter took it from him with a grunt and peered at the price tag.

"What's going on at the church?" Hugh asked, knowing that he'd probably be happier without that information—yet somehow unable to help himself.

The proprietor let out a deeper, more disapproving grunt and rang up the vodka. "Nellie from the bakery says someone called in a bomb threat, of all the daft things," he said. "It's all a load of old rot, I'm sure."

Hugh found it endlessly confounding that people still casually dismissed such things in the face of, well, *everything*. Yet he found the idea of humanity's madness reaching this little oasis of calm upsetting on a deeply personal level.

"No doubt you're right. I hope so, anyway," he said, handing over the money and waving away the offer of change. He took his purchase and wished the old man a good day, eager to get back to the cottage and get this whole fiasco over with.

By the time he returned to the crossroads, the intersection was completely blocked off. At the direction of a grim-faced police officer, he awkwardly turned the van around and backtracked. This required a ridiculously long detour to get back to where he needed to be. By the time he made his way onto the narrow, one-lane road leading to his property, he was worried and irritated in equal measure.

Even with the added driving, it hadn't been *that* long, but still... Phobetor's shadowy influence pricked at him, whispering about all the things that could have happened while he was gone.

In reality, he barged into the cottage to find Morpheus and Iridaceae in the kitchen, more or less where he'd left them. Some of the tension drained from his shoulders, but not before Morpheus frowned, rising from his chair.

"You are upset," he said. "Has something happened?"

"No," Hugh said quickly. "No, everything's fine." He took the vodka out of his shopping bag and set it on the table. "Come on, let's do this. No point in procrastinating."

Suiting action to word, he fetched a chair and got down to serious drinking. He'd forgotten how much cheap vodka burned going down. Normally, there might have been a pleasant-ish stretch between starting to drink and getting sloppy drunk, but in his current mindset, the alcohol just made him increasingly depressed and paranoid.

The woebegone look Morpheus was giving him didn't help matters very much. Nor did the thought that occurred to him about halfway through the bottle.

"Wait," he said. "Can dead souls be drunk?"

Because that could be awkward when he needed to relay a message to a god, preferably without slurring it into incomprehensibility.

"No, Hugh," Morpheus said patiently, though he was still wearing the same unhappy, pinched expression. "There are many reasons why this may not work; however, that is not one of them."

Hugh blinked at him and took another swig from the bottle, before setting it down with a bit more force than he'd intended. "Don' be sush a d... downer."

He blinked again. That had sounded drunk to his own ears. He tipped the bottle up to his lips, chugging and trying not to cough. It had only been about ten minutes, but the alcohol was already hitting his bloodstream. He needed to get the rest of the bottle down before he lost too much coordination to manage it.

"Should've introduced him to Dionysus before he locked down his realm," Iridaceae muttered, watching him drink in fascination.

Morpheus didn't answer. Hugh wanted to ask a question — *several* questions — but it suddenly felt like too much effort. He set the bottle down, it wavered and fell onto its side with a heavy clink, rolling toward the edge. Morpheus rescued it before it could fall to the floor and moved it to the counter by the stove.

Hugh set his head down on his arms, but it did nothing to stop the room spinning. "Don' feel so good," he told the tabletop.

"Shocking," Morpheus' voice came from just behind him. A slender hand grasped his bicep. "Come. We should get you to the bathroom. I suspect you'll have need of a convenient porcelain receptacle at some point during this distasteful process."

He was probably right. Hugh tried to help as Morpheus and Iridaceae hauled him to his feet and supported his staggering form down the hallway.

He was vaguely aware that someone had placed a folded blanket and a pillow on the cold bathroom floor between the bathtub and the toilet. His surroundings lurched unpleasantly as they lowered him onto the makeshift bed… and so did his stomach.

Morpheus sank down to sit cross-legged next to him, taking one of Hugh's hands in his. And that was… nice. He'd lost track of the clock, but his body was already succumbing to too much alcohol in far too short a time. He felt sick and confused, and none of his limbs seemed to be properly attached to his body anymore.

A cool hand stroked the hair back from his forehead, and that was nice, too. Nothing else felt *at all* nice, though, and Hugh wondered idly if alcohol poisoning would be enough to take him out all on its own.

He couldn't hold onto the thought. He couldn't hold onto much of *anything*. But his surroundings were growing dark and far away, so maybe it didn't matter. The roiling of his stomach became distant and unimportant. The relief that maybe he wasn't going to throw up while lying helplessly on his back followed him down into damp, sweaty darkness.

⸺◆⸺

Morpheus forced himself to stay and watch while Iridaceae pressed a pillow over Hugh's slack face. He wasn't certain what his own expression looked like as Hugh's body twitched and jerked in the depths of its unconsciousness, but his familiar scowled up at him.

"Stop it," she said, evidently capable of multitasking while casually murdering a human. "He said we could do it, and he'll come right back afterward. He always does."

Hugh's right arm flailed weakly upward, too uncoordinated to grasp the pillow smothering his airways. A heavy wave of combined nausea, anger, and irrational fear sent Morpheus' stomach tossing in a way it hadn't since his first awful days as a mortal.

"I wish Phobetor dead," he realized, barely aware that he'd spoken the words aloud. "My own brother. If I had the power, I would see him obliterated from the universe for all time."

Iridaceae looked up at him, still holding the pillow in place as Hugh's body gave up its weak struggle for air. Morpheus knew that, if he were still a god, he'd have felt the human's vibrant subconscious subside into a low, monotone hum as his life force fled.

"Could the mortal realm survive without fear?" his familiar asked.

"I do not know," Morpheus said, alarmed to find that he also did not *care*.

Iridaceae frowned, turning her attention back to her victim. Holding the pillow with one hand, she grasped Hugh's wrist with the other. "I can't feel a pulse."

She lifted the pillow away cautiously, but no breath lifted Hugh's chest. With a satisfied nod, she set the pillow aside and settled in with her back resting against the free-standing bathtub.

"I guess now we just wait," she said.

They waited.

Morpheus did not doubt that Thanatus would travel to his side with all alacrity upon learning that he wished to collect on his promised favor. It was, however, no surprise to him at all when his uncle failed to appear as minutes passed, stretching into an hour, and then two.

Iridaceae remained stubbornly silent, her arms crossed… unwilling to voice what they both knew. It hadn't worked.

Hugh's ribcage spasmed and rose, pulling in a rasping breath. Remembering something the human had warned him about during his first days of violent sickness, Morpheus tugged him onto his side and resettled him there, to reduce the possibility of aspiration should he be ill while still unconscious.

From previous experience, Morpheus was unsure whether Hugh would regain awareness quickly, or whether it would take time for his body to clear the alcohol even though it had already repaired the damage due to oxygen starvation.

As minutes passed and Hugh's breathing steadied, there remained no sign of consciousness.

"It may take him some time to recover fully," Morpheus said. "Even so, I believe we can conclude that he was unsuccessful in communicating with Thanatus."

Alarm flitted across Iridaceae's pixielike features. "You can't know that for sure! We should wait for Hugh to wake up and tell us what happened.

Maybe he learned something this time, and we can try again—"

A deafening explosion rumbled across the landscape, followed a second later by a shock wave that rattled the walls of the ancient cottage. Iridaceae yelped in alarm. Some unknown instinct had Morpheus grabbing her and pulling her to lie over Hugh, while he hunched over both of them, trying to shield them with his body. Fine plaster dust sprinkled down from the ceiling, and Morpheus fought not to let his mind slide back to a human bunker collapsing beneath unseen aerial bombardment.

"What the hell was *that*?" Iridaceae squeaked, clutching at him.

TWENTY-FIVE

"I DON'T KNOW," Morpheus said, even as his mind whispered, *'a bomb, it's a bomb, we are not safe here.'*

He remained huddled over the shaking form of his familiar and the unresponsive body of his lover, every muscle pulled as taut as a drawn bowstring. Seconds passed, marked only by his stuttering heartbeat. The seconds became minutes. No more explosions followed.

"I think you can let me up now," Iridaceae said. Her voice was tiny and hesitant, but her birdlike trembling had stilled by degrees as it became obvious that they were not under a sustained direct attack.

"Yes," Morpheus said, although he had to force his limbs to loosen and his back to straighten. Had the explosion been nearby and relatively small, or had it been far away and exponentially larger?

His thoughts raced, replaying the litany of recounted horrors from the news reports he'd read on Hugh's computer. In the distance, sirens wailed—their pitch rising and falling in a Doppler effect as they grew closer, only to pass by and continue on, receding fast.

Larger and farther away, then, it seemed… but still close enough to intrude directly on the little oasis of tranquility Hugh had built for himself.

Iridaceae frowned down at the unmoving human, grasping his shoulder and shaking it roughly.

"Wake up," she said. "Something bad is happening and we don't know what it is! Hugh, wake *up!*"

Hugh lolled limply beneath her grip, still deeply unconscious. He would not be waking up anytime soon.

All at once, Morpheus knew what he must do. Or rather, he knew that he must act *now*, before Hugh regained awareness. He'd known from the beginning that this was what would ultimately be required of him.

The dissolution of human society was no longer a faraway, theoretical concept. It was happening all around them, throwing innocent mortal lives into chaos, terror, and death while he lay in a comfortable bed, ate good food, and visited the local countryside for his own enjoyment.

It was time to do what must be done, before additional temptation to wait — to put off the inevitable for another hour, another day, another week — further softened his shaky resolve.

The way forward solidified in his consciousness between one breath and the next. He rose on unsteady legs.

"Come," he told Iridaceae. "I think I know where we can find something that will help."

She shot an uncertain look at Hugh, and then at him. "What kind of something?"

"I'll show you," he said, refusing to allow guilt to take hold. He headed down the hall toward the kitchen, Iridaceae's hesitant footsteps trailing behind him.

The cottage was old. Perhaps not as old as its occupant, but certainly predating many of the detailed health and safety regulations that constrained modern residential construction.

"I'm certain I saw smelling salts around here earlier," he said, opening a random cabinet and pretending to study its contents. "We need to wake Hugh as quickly as possible."

"Smelling salts?" Iridaceae echoed, in a tone of skepticism. "Do humans still use those?"

"Remember whose dwelling this is," Morpheus said, injecting the words with wryness. He opened another cabinet, then glanced over his shoulder at his companion. "Check inside the pantry, please. I'll search the shelves and cabinets."

Iridaceae gave him another odd look, but she had been his creature for far too long. Obeying him was second nature to her. After a moment's hesitation, she slipped into the closet-like room tucked into a corner of the kitchen.

"It was a small glass vial with a white label," Morpheus called after her. "I believe it had a cork stopper."

When the sound of rustling and clinking emerged from inside the small space, Morpheus stepped silently to the pantry door and closed it. He had noted previously, while watching Hugh move around the kitchen preparing meals, that the door locked from the outside with an old-fashioned key; one which always remained in the mechanism. Ignoring Iridaceae's startled squawk of outrage, he turned the key until the lock clicked, then pulled it free and laid it in plain view on the counter next to the door.

Something inside clattered to the floor, and the door rattled as the knob twisted back and forth fruitlessly.

"What are you *doing*?" Iridaceae cried, the words shot through with betrayal. "*Morpheus!*"

"I am doing what we both know must be done," he said, and went to find a suitably long and sharp knife from the wooden block next to the sink.

The door rattled harder. "No, don't! Just wait, *please!*"

Knowing that his time was limited—the lock wasn't *that* strong—he chose a slender boning knife and left without answering. The newly repaired front door of the cottage opened smoothly to his touch on well-oiled hinges, and then closed behind him with a soft sound of finality.

Perhaps it would have made more sense to act immediately rather than going outside first, but somehow the prospect of bleeding all over the floor of Hugh's home made his stomach twist unpleasantly.

He made his way into the dense stand of trees surrounding the modest cottage. If he was quick enough with his errand, the others might not find this damaged vessel of flesh hidden in the forest before he was successful in gaining Thanatus' help and returning.

He ducked between thick trunks and the smaller, grasping branches of underbrush until he reached a tiny clearing—the legacy of a fallen tree that had torn branches from its brethren on its way down. He glanced up, taking in the small patch of gray clouds visible overhead. The air around him was damp and heavy despite the morning chill still clinging to it. Perhaps it would rain soon.

When he lowered his gaze to his immediate surroundings again, a black cat with a tattered ear sat crouched on the hollow trunk of the fallen tree, blinking at him with large, yellow eyes.

"Baphometh," Morpheus greeted. "Hello. This is rather awkward, isn't it? Although, as you are not a dog, I trust you won't lead Hugh and Iridaceae back to this place when I am done. Doing so would upset them."

Baphometh continued to stare at him in a rather disconcerting manner. All too aware that his time was limited, Morpheus turned his back on the animal, putting its presence out of his mind. He placed the knife on the damp loam at his feet and straightened, grasping the hem of his knitted jumper and the undershirt beneath, lifting both items of clothing over his head at once.

Muscle and sinew pulled and shifted beneath his mortal skin; the sensation always so visceral compared to what he'd been used to for most of his existence. But he could not afford to mourn the loss of this odd time out of time... this stretch of days when he had no longer been the God of the Sleeping Mind, but merely one man cherished and loved by another.

He tossed the clothes aside and retrieved the blade. Hugh was, as he so often said, still a medieval peasant at heart. He knew the value of a finely honed edge. The knife was slender and very slightly curved, wickedly sharp at the point. While it lacked a proper crossguard, the handle flared wider at the tang, enough to prevent careless fingers from sliding forward onto the blade.

Straightening his spine, Morpheus turned the point toward his torso, placing it between this body's fourth and fifth ribs, just to the left of the costal cartilage, angled slightly upward and inward.

"You could have made this whole thing considerably simpler, Uncle," he said to the empty air. Then he drew a deep breath, steeled himself, and thrust the knife deep.

———◆———

Hugh jerked awake and flopped onto his back with a groan, staring up at a crack in the plaster of the bathroom ceiling that he was reasonably sure hadn't been there before he'd blacked out.

His pulse thudded in his ears, seeming unnaturally loud until he realized that the sound was not, in fact, that of his own heartbeat. It was the sound of someone pounding against something... probably something made of wood. His head throbbed in a way that suggested his eyeballs might explode at any moment, and his mouth tasted like stomach acid.

There was something important he was supposed to remember.

Whatever it was, he didn't remember it.

He must've been dead. That was the usual explanation for this stretch of utter, blank nothingness in his memory. The problem was, he was fairly certain he'd expected the experience to be different this time.

Why was that?

The pounding grew louder, now accompanied by an ominous splintering noise.

"I hate you! *I hate you!*" The hoarse, muffled cries had him lunging into a sitting position and immediately regretting it. "Gods and goddesses!" continued the familiar voice. *"Why are you like this?"*

Hugh clutched his head and tried not to pass out again as the room spun around him. An even louder crash—one with an air of finality to it—echoed through his pounding skull like a struck gong with edges made of razor blades.

Running footsteps thudded down the hall, and Iridaceae caught herself on the bathroom doorframe, sliding to an ungainly stop. Not even Hugh's watering eyes and swimming vision could hide the high flush reddening her face and the tear tracks streaming down her cheeks.

"Hugh!" she sobbed. "I couldn't stop him! I'm so sorry—I tried! *I couldn't stop him!*"

Hugh stared at her, and not even the stabbing pain of a death-hangover could stop the bottom from falling out of his world with horrible, swooping finality.

TWENTY-SIX

THE DARKNESS OF nonexistence was more complete and all-consuming than the deepest void of outer space. The wisp of remembered life that had once been Morpheus felt surprise at this. He had not expected it to be so.

Just as he had been able to recognize landmarks in his brothers' realms when he had gone in search of Hugh inside the prison of Hallucination, he had expected to recognize the familiar environs of Tartarus. He had plotted with great precision the route he would take to reach Thanatus' castle, perched precariously among the cliffs of Perdition.

He knew well what areas he would have to avoid — the Cave of Hypnos, the River Lethe… anything that might sap away the memory of his purpose here. The image of the route had been clear as daylight in his mind, traversing places he'd visited many times before.

The soul that had once been Morpheus had assumed that he would experience his uncle's realm in the same way a god experienced it.

He had been wrong.

The pit was unending and directionless. In the fathomless distance, something unimaginably large and unimaginably angry was screaming in rage. The thing which had been Morpheus remembered with trepidation the monsters that called this endless lacuna their prison.

Creatures so vast they crumbled mountains beneath their twisted bodies — grotesque offspring of the Old Gods. Reviled even by their progenitors, who had trapped them here for eternity after the great wars of the distant past.

The Cyclopes. The Hundred-Handers. Titans that could crush a minor god of Morpheus' ilk with ease, and to whom a defenseless mortal soul would be the merest puff of air, consumed and expelled effortlessly with a single breath.

The wailing cries rose in volume, fury and despair made palpable. What remained of Morpheus shuddered in existential dread.

The pit was where souls went for judgment. Had he been a good person during his ageless existence? Fresh panic vibrated through the formless remnant which was all that remained of him.

He was quite certain that he had not been.

This was not right. This was not why he was *here*. There was something else... something important.

The utter darkness surrounding him jostled his insubstantial form like a crowd of mortals fleeing an explosion in a nineteenth century town square. High-pitched, grating laughter battered at his senses.

Little godling, jeered a rasping voice. *Why are you here, little godling?*

Godling.

Yes. He was here... to see a god.

He was here to see his *uncle*.

He tried to form words, but he was made of shadows and nothing. The hysterical laughter rose higher.

The weight of your sins is drawing you down into the pit, sing-songed the voice. *Soon, the monsters will take you! Unless…*

The remnant of Morpheus latched onto that final, trailing word.

Unless…?

You could become a shade like us… and serve the God of Death forevermore! The cackling rose to a crescendo of deranged mirth.

Shades. The creatures swirling around him and enveloping him in darkness were *shades.* Souls that refused to pass into judgment, cursed instead to linger in the between places. They were Tartarus' equivalent of his own oneiri—existing only in service to Thanatus, just as the oneiri had once served *him.*

The enraged roaring from below had grown so loud that it vibrated through him as though it would rip him into his constituent subatomic particles. The remnant that had been Morpheus knew with abrupt conviction that the weight of his sins would never allow him to rise above the pit of judgment.

With sudden desperation, he grasped clumsily for the darkness surrounding him, reaching out for it with everything he had left. It was not, at this point, very much.

Oooh, it wants to become like us! crooned the shade. *It wants to serve the master forever!*

A sensation like clammy hands stroking him made him flinch inward, trying to cringe away. But there *was* no 'away.'

Make it like us! Make it like us! chorused the voices.

The blackness that had surrounded him since he'd regained what passed for awareness plunged deeper into him, swirling together with whatever constituted his essence until he could not tell where he ended, and it began.

It was cold… *so very cold.*

Cold like a collapsed bunker. Like an Edinburgh morgue.

How could anything be so *cold*?

If you wanted to be warm, you should have burned in the flames at the bottom of the pit! the voice shrieked in vicious glee. *It's warm in the lake of fire!*

As the cold and the dark took him over, it lent him a solidity he hadn't possessed before. Or perhaps *solidity* wasn't the word.

Continuity.

Tangibility.

The shades would make poor servants indeed without a bit of metaphysical heft to lend them agency.

A hint of his purpose here returned. The shade who had been Morpheus realized that he'd been doomed to sink into the pit from the start. Those who exercised power over others weaker than themselves always were—and as a god, he had been more powerful than most.

I must present myself to my new master, he communicated to his fellow shades.

He is not here! He is not here! they chanted. *Our master has gone to the mortal realm!*

The mortal realm? Truly? If his uncle had finally decided to act in response to Phobetor's vile machinations just as Morpheus had killed himself to reach

Tartarus, he was going to have some strong words for the God of Death.

Then I must present myself at our master's palace and wait for him to return, he conveyed.

Yes, follow, follow! the shades said, herding him along in a direction that he sincerely hoped was 'up.'

Below them, the monsters cried out in frustration as their prize was chivvied away.

------------◆------------

Like the rest of Tartarus, Thanatus' palace was almost unrecognizable to him in this form. It was like being inside a smudged pencil drawing of death's stronghold—flat and grainy and unreal.

Some small part of him remembered flashes of warmth and color... of lying in a bed with dawn light streaming through window curtains, a lover's body pressed to his back. Already, it was becoming difficult to bring forward the details of emotion and sensation. A fresh chill shuddered through the darkness that now encompassed his existence at the prospect of losing those memories completely.

The shades shoved him into a bare stone chamber and receded to hover in the shadows at the edges of the space, tittering amongst themselves. The frozen darkness that had once been Morpheus floated there, chasing a sense that he should try to reach a different room... the throne room?

Yet the niggling desire to leave could not overcome the increasing weight of his inertia. How could he reach this *throne room*? Would he even recognize it if he somehow stumbled across it by sheer chance?

It was so much easier to let time slide over him in a meaningless trickle, watching parts of his past spool away into nothingness like vapor sublimating from a chunk of dry ice.

Eventually, one of the shades lurking near the chamber door darted away with an excited squeal, disappearing into the corridor beyond. Moments later, it returned, tugging at the robes of a towering figure like a child dragging a reluctant parent toward a circus tent.

It's a very powerful one, Your Grace! it was saying. *The most powerful one we have seen in ages! It was falling into the pit, too heavy to right itself. It wanted to become like us!*

"Let's see it, then," came a deep voice.

The familiar figure approached, and unlike everything else in this two-dimensional, pencil-drawn existence, it was viscerally and undeniably *real*. The shade that had been Morpheus swayed forward, drawn to the God of Death like iron filings to a magnet. He would follow this god. He would pledge his service to this being who called to the ice and darkness inside him. He would—

Thanatus loomed over him, scowling down at his cowering form. He saw the moment when the God of Death's obsidian eyes widened in shock. For an instant, he couldn't imagine why he would evince such a reaction from a being so powerful and perfect.

"What... is the meaning of this?" Thanatus thundered.

Every shade in the chamber fled in terror, leaving vaporous black trails in their wake. Every shade... except Morpheus.

Morpheus twisted, trying to become smaller — to disappear into the flagstone floor.

"You *fool!*" Thanatus raged. "What have you *done?*"

The furious question sparked something inside Morpheus' rapidly unraveling mind. He had done something. What had he done?

I... committed suicide, he realized. *I needed to come here. I had to... ask you...*

Thanatus stalked around him in a circle, anger rolling off him in heavy waves. "You absolute *idiot!* That bird of yours told me what you allowed to happen, but never in an *eternity* would I believe you stupid enough to do *this!*"

I had to ask you... Morpheus repeated doggedly, with no idea of what the question was supposed to have been. He hesitated, flashes of faces and snippets of memory strobing rapid-fire through his fractured awareness.

That bird of yours...

Elfin features. Soft feathers.

A tiny, pale opal nestled in the hollow of her neck.

Connections slotted into place. An opal. A missing opal. Only one way to get it back.

I wish to claim the favor owed to me, he gasped out in a rush.

"The *favor!*" Thanatus spat. "You come here to me, like this, to claim your *winnings?*"

Yes, he said, falling to lie prostrate on the floor beneath the force of his new master's rage. *I claim what is mine, by rite of honor.*

Above him, Thanatus snarled in fury.

TWENTY-SEVEN

A BLACK HAZE SWIRLED around Thanatus' towering form—the same utter absence of light as the depths of the pit where the Titans were caged in their inescapable prison. The shade that had been Morpheus felt his pitiful essence unraveling with terrifying speed under the weight of the God of Death's disapproval.

Then, a dark hand reached down and plucked him from his ignominious position on the stone floor, dragging him up like a human scruffing a helpless kitten. Thanatus' eyes were lost in the void of shadow beneath his thunderous brows.

With a noise of disgust, the God of Death channeled voidstuff through the point of physical contact between them. The fading echo of Morpheus felt himself filling out, gaining mass… becoming *real*. With a gasp, he came fully back to himself, appalled by how close he'd come to nonexistence.

Thanatus set him down with a sneer—still a pathetic and insubstantial thing, even with the return of his wits.

"You wish to redeem your *favor*," he spat. "Very well. *Speak*."

As the influx of his uncle's power pulled Morpheus back from the brink, so too did the events of the last few weeks come crashing back into his awareness.

I wish you to recover the stolen opal necklace containing my godhood from Phobetor and return its contents to me. He paused, attempting to ensure there were no loopholes in his request that might prevent him from achieving his goal. *I require you to assist me in returning to my proper position as the God of Dreams and Nightmares, as I was before voluntarily becoming mortal.*

Anger still rolled off Thanatus in dark, vaporous waves. "In other words, you require me to shield you from the consequences of your own foolish choices."

Morpheus remained silent. He refused to regret the actions he had taken to save Hugh from the clutches of his treacherous brothers. He *refused.*

Thanatus glared down at him. "I once regarded you with affection, son of my sibling. Honor demands my compliance with your request, but from this day forward, you are no nephew of mine."

You speak of my choices, Morpheus replied... unwisely, perhaps. *But what of my brother's choices? Phobetor is the one who trampled the old laws regarding interference in the Sublunary. Will you turn your eyes away, simply because his reign of terror in the mortal realm reaps more souls for your dark kingdom?*

For the barest moment, Thanatus appeared discomfited. He rocked back a few inches, the weight of his displeasure receding for an instant before returning in force.

"Come," he rumbled, grasping Morpheus' insubstantial wraith-form once more. "You would do well not to insult the only god in the firmament who owes you a debt."

Without ceremony, Thanatus swept him into the folds of his black robes, as though he were nothing more than a silk kerchief or a small parcel. Panic clawed at Morpheus as he was subsumed by the power of the god who ruled all shades. Between one instant and the next, he had become nothing more than a voiceless passenger. With what paltry agency he still possessed gone, he could only hope that Thanatus would follow through with both the letter and the spirit of his request.

———◆———

Morpheus felt the shift as the veil between realms parted beneath Thanatus' touch. But instead of the Sublunary, they stepped into Phantasos' airy palace. He watched through his uncle's senses as the God of Fantasy rose from his throne in surprise. Around him, the tangle of nubile flesh that had been giggling and stroking him parted as he stepped down from the fur-and velvet-strewn dais.

"Uncle! I was not expecting a visit," Phantasos said. "If I'd known you were coming, I would've had a proper welcome waiting for you…"

He trailed off, pausing a few steps away as though noticing Thanatus' severe expression for the first time. The God of Death closed the distance in two long strides and grasped Phantasos by the throat, slamming him against a nearby pillar carved with nymphs and satyrs.

"Take me to your brother," he said. "*Now.*"

Phantasos spluttered, clawing ineffectually at the iron hand circling his neck. "What are you *on* about?" he yelped. "Unhand me, Uncle!"

Thanatus thumped him against the pillar again for good measure, with more force this time. "The next words out of your smarmy mouth will be '*Yes, Uncle, I'll take you to him immediately,*' or I will toss your useless carcass into the pit with the Cyclopes for the next thousand years."

Phantasos gaped at him, the alluring brown eyes that had inspired a thousand sonnets bulging in their sockets. Fear flared behind his shocked gaze.

"Yes, Uncle," he said meekly. "I'll… um… I'll take you to him right now."

Thanatus released his grip and brushed imaginary dust off the slender, golden-haired youth's shoulders. "How *kind* of you, Nephew." His voice dripped sarcasm.

Still staring at Thanatus in shock, Phantasos made a show of stretching the kinks out of his neck and squaring his shoulders. "He's in the Sublunary. Working on a project that will benefit *you* as much — if not more — than the rest of us." Resentment colored the words.

Thanatus made an ironic 'after you' gesture with one hand. Phantasos gave him a final sidelong look of bewilderment and stepped through the veil. The God of Death followed him.

They emerged halfway up on the side of a mountain in the mortal realm. Snow covered the jutting rocks, and above them, the sky was an unlikely shade of robin's egg blue. Explosions and gunfire rocked the valley below, interspersed with human screams as two ragtag armies clashed in an effusion of smoke and blood.

On a nearby flat-topped boulder sat Phobetor, hunched like a gangly spider as he watched the carnage unfolding below. The same surge of visceral hatred Morpheus had experienced toward his brother at Hugh's cottage returned with a vengeance. Had he possessed a body, he would have been hard-pressed not to lunge forward and attack the God of Fear physically.

"Well," said the embodiment of all Morpheus' woes, "This is certainly an unexpected pleasure. Good day, Uncle. Good day, Brother. What can I do for you?"

Phantasos looked highly uncomfortable. "Sorry, Phobetor. He made me bring him here. I don't know why."

"I require the opal necklace you stole," Thanatus said flatly. "Hand it over, and we'll be on our way."

Phobetor's eyes widened in a caricature of innocent surprise that sat poorly on his gaunt face. "An opal necklace? I'm sure I have no idea what you mean."

Thanatus growled and reached inside his robes, grasping Morpheus' insubstantial remains and flinging him onto the snowy ground at Phobetor's feet.

"My patience today is already exhausted, you detestable little vulture," Thanatus snarled. "I have no tolerance for your games."

The God of Fear sat frozen, staring at Morpheus for an endless moment. Then, he burst into vicious, cackling laughter.

"Oh! Oh, my!" he gasped, overcome with merriment. "Now *this* was worth the price of admission, a hundred times over! My milquetoast brother, reduced to a mindless shade?" He doubled over, clutching his stomach as he guffawed.

Thanatus lifted a hand, darkness unfurling in a sinuous wave from his palm. The voidstuff billowed across the distance separating them and wrapped around Phobetor's limbs like hungry snakes. With a sharp jerk, Thanatus dragged Phobetor off his perch and pinned him next to where Morpheus' ethereal form lay in a tangled heap.

Even constricted by the God of Death's bondage, Phobetor continued to wheeze out breathless peals of laughter. Thanatus stretched down and grabbed Morpheus once again, stuffing him back inside his robes. Morpheus felt his uncle reach *through* him, searching out the connection to the opal containing his lost powers.

With a twitch of his fingers, Thanatus called forth the pendant, which ripped a hole through the pocket of Phobetor's drab jacket and flew directly into his hand.

"Your reach exceeds your grasp, Phobetor," he said. "Have a care, before someone loses patience and slices your arm off."

With that, he stepped back, returning through the veil to his palace on the Cliffs of Perdition. Without ceremony, he pulled Morpheus out and threw him to the floor, then tossed the opal onto him. It sank into the shadowy darkness of his shade body, and Morpheus grasped frantically for the essence it contained.

It burst through him in a wave of ecstatic relief, rushing into all the aching places that had been burned away by mortality and death. For a few giddy moments, he merely lay there, basking in the return of his power. When he came back to himself, he rose to his feet, pulling his preferred physical form together around his consciousness like a comfortable cloak.

Dark breeches, tall boots, a white silk shirt, and a formal, knee-length embroidered coat in midnight blue settled over his newly reformed skin. His awareness expanded outward, twining together with the mortals' collective unconscious like the branches of a fast-growing tree interweaving with its neighbors in a forest.

A heartfelt sigh bowed his shoulders; his chin dropped to his chest.

"The debt is paid," Thanatus said heavily. "Now get out of my lands. I have no desire to see you or either of your ne'er-do-well brothers for the foreseeable future."

Morpheus looked up at his uncle. The wise thing would be to heed his words and leave. Unfortunately, Morpheus' track record with wise decisions had been severely lacking, as of late.

"Uncle," he said. "What has happened to us?"

"What do you mean?" Thanatus sounded suddenly tired, as though the effort of forming the words was exhausting.

"Our family," Morpheus clarified. "We were not always like this. What happened?"

Thanatus stared at him, his earlier anger giving way to a deep melancholy. "Nothing that can be repaired," was all he said.

Morpheus continued to hold his gaze for a long moment, but it was obvious Thanatus had nothing more to say on the subject.

"I see," Morpheus told him, even though it was a lie. "In that case, I will take my leave as you have asked. You have my thanks."

The urge to return directly to his own realm and check on the state of things tugged at him, but he set the compulsion aside with difficulty. There was something more important he had to do first.

TWENTY-EIGHT

I'M GOING TO KILL him, Hugh thought, before realizing how ridiculous that sounded, even inside his own head. *Okay, I'm going to* punch *him. I will knock a tooth out of that goddamned pretty face, even if I have to do it posthumously.*

"There was a great big explosion," Iridaceae was saying. "It rattled the house, and then there were police sirens, and we didn't know what was happening, and you were still unconscious!"

The run-on sentence staggered to an ungainly end, even as Iridaceae swayed under the weight of Hugh's heavy arm across her narrow shoulders. She dragged him in an unsteady zigzag down the hallway, where Hugh's feet crunched over yet more fallen bits of ceiling plaster.

"An explosion…" he said stupidly, cursing the fact that he was still fucking *drunk*, on top of everything else. His tongue felt thick and ungainly.

An explosion, with sirens?

Someone called in a bomb threat, of all the daft things. The memory of the shopkeeper's words felt like something that had happened a decade ago, rather than a scant few hours. *It's all a load of old rot, I'm sure.*

Had Hugh's sleepy little English village been wiped completely off the map? Was everyone dead? What kind of bomb had it *been*?

Dead.

He'd been dead, but he had no memory of seeing Thanatus, much less speaking to him. Hugh had failed, and the village had exploded, and now Morpheus had run off to do the thing Hugh had been terrified about all along.

His head pounded; the pain so intense that dying again of an uncontrolled brain bleed seemed like a valid concern. Iridaceae steered him into the kitchen, where he had a confused impression of a very small tornado having demolished his pantry door.

"He told me we needed to find smelling salts to wake you," Iridaceae said. "He said I should look in the pantry, and then he locked me in!" Her tone sounded deeply affronted, and she shook her head sharply. "Anyway, I think he went out the front door."

Hugh tried to take more of his own weight, struggling to think logically as his feet stumbled over themselves. Did Morpheus know where Hugh kept his shotgun? Would he know how to load it, how to use it? Even if he did, killing yourself with a long-barreled gun wasn't a straightforward proposition. He'd need string to tie to the trigger…

"Have there been any other loud noises since the explosion?" he asked thickly. "Gunshots?"

"No," Iridaceae said. "I haven't heard anything since the front door opened and closed." She paused. "Mind you, I *was* kicking down the pantry door for a good part of that time. It made things a bit noisy."

"I'd noticed," Hugh replied, his skull still pulsing agony in time with the memory of splintering wood.

Christ... if Morpheus had gone outside, how were they going to find him?

They reached the front door—closed, but not locked. Hugh forced himself to stop leaning on Iridaceae's petite frame. His knees felt like water, but that had less to do with the alcohol poisoning and more to do with what he feared to find outside.

Iridaceae opened the door and they both rushed out.

"The van," Hugh said. "Are the van and the bicycle still here?"

They were. Hugh felt a tiny flash of relief. If Morpheus had figured out how to drive the van, he could have been anywhere by now. The bicycle was slower, but it would still have given him a huge head start. As it was, he had to be within walking distance of the cottage.

"I'll check 'round the back," Iridaceae said tightly. "You know, wings would be *really* useful, right about now."

As far as Hugh was concerned, some functioning neurons would have been really useful right about now, too—but beggars couldn't be choosers. Iridaceae ran off, disappearing behind the cottage and emerging a few seconds later.

"He's not there!" she said, breathless.

Think! Think, think, think, damn it...

"You're an owl," Hugh said. "Go hunting."

She looked confused for a moment, then brightened. "A trail! He's mortal—he would have left a trail!"

A chilly gust of wind brought the scent of rain with it, a few fitful drops spattering against Hugh's face. It had been damp enough for the last couple of weeks that footprints should show up, at least once a person left the gravel and thick sod surrounding the cottage.

Hugh and Iridaceae split up, heading in opposite directions. Hugh made himself focus on the ground despite his swimming head, calling up skills learned hundreds of years ago, when tracking game in the forest could mean the difference between eating and going hungry.

He'd covered maybe fifty feet at the edge of the woods when Iridaceae cried out.

"Over here!"

Hugh hurried toward the shout, finding her staring into the forest, her hand braced against a scrawny tree trunk. It wasn't a proper path, but there was a gap in the underbrush large enough for a slender person to traverse. A bare patch where the leaf litter was sparse enough to reveal the soft earth beneath showed the angular indentation of a shoe heel.

"Got you," Hugh whispered. Then, louder, "Morpheus! *Morpheus*! Don't you *dare* do anything stupid, damn you!"

Iridaceae darted into the gap, and Hugh forced his way after her. Brambles grasped at his sleeves, scraping his hands and forearms. The wind rattled leafy branches above them, a few more raindrops reaching the ground through the forest canopy.

Iridaceae was on the proverbial scent, now... following a trail of bent branches and faint footprints. They took turns calling out to Morpheus, alternately begging him and threatening dire punishments if he did anything before they caught up to him.

Ahead, the quality of the light changed, murky shadows giving way to a lighter gray. *A clearing.* Iridaceae gasped and crashed to a halt so abruptly that Hugh bumped into her back, steadying himself with a hand on her shoulder.

Queasy with dread, he squeezed through to stand next to her, looking down at the still figure crumpled on the ground by a large, downed tree trunk.

Morpheus lay where he had fallen, his body bare to the waist. His pale skin was translucent, tinged blue gray except for the tacky river of drying crimson seeping down the contour of his left pectoral.

The handle of Hugh's best kitchen knife protruded obscenely from between his ribs. Incongruously, Hugh's raggedy black tomcat sat primly on the dip of Morpheus' right shoulder, his tail curled in a fastidious loop over his paws. He blinked up at the newcomers as though accusing them of being late to a dinner party.

"*Mreow,*" he said, a bit plaintively.

Hugh wasn't certain how his legs got him from the edge of the clearing to Morpheus' side. There was a short, blank pause, and then he was falling to his knees next to the unmoving body. His hand shook as he reached out to press two fingers beneath the sharply defined jaw, already knowing what he would find.

Or rather, what he wouldn't.

Iridaceae lowered herself to kneel next to him. Baphometh meowed again and butted his head against her shoulder, his ears flicking back in distaste when the rain began to fall in earnest.

Hugh stared as the droplets splattered against the congealing trail of heart's blood, diluting it like turpentine dribbled on oil paint.

"I told him to wait," Iridaceae whispered.

"And I am sorry I could not," said a voice from the other side of the small clearing.

Very slowly, Hugh looked up from the dead, cooling body of Morpheus, to see… *Morpheus*. He was standing perhaps fifteen feet away, looking as beautiful and untouchable as he ever had—clad in the finery of an eccentric nineteenth century gentleman.

The rain didn't even seem to touch him.

Next to Hugh, Iridaceae sagged in relief. "Oh," she said. "I guess it worked, then."

"It did," Morpheus agreed, crossing to join them with silent footfalls.

"I'm still angry at you," Iridaceae said, a quaver running beneath the words.

"I know," Morpheus told her, gazing down at the corpse with a faint frown.

Baphometh hissed half-heartedly as Morpheus reached a hand down to draw Hugh to his feet. Hugh allowed himself to be drawn, incandescent rage bubbling up from his stomach and exploding through his chest. Silent concern creased Morpheus' chiseled features as they faced each other in the drizzling rain.

Blood rushed through Hugh's ears in a deafening torrent. He jerked free of Morpheus' supporting grip—clenching his fist... drawing it back in readiness to deliver the punishing blow he'd promised himself. The blow that would make Morpheus hurt the same way Hugh's heart hurt.

Crystalline blue eyes swam in his vision, shining with regret and remorse. Hugh's vision blurred, burning pressure overflowing into salty trails of heat on his cheeks. His raised arm trembled, and somehow, he was toppling forward... crashing into a lithe form that caught him and held him fast with unnatural strength.

"Shh," Morpheus said. "I am here. I have not left you."

"Goddamn you," Hugh choked into the crook of Morpheus' neck. "God*damn* you!"

Cool arms wrapped around his shoulders, holding him close as he clutched handfuls of midnight-blue brocade and buried his face against a god's pale throat.

TWENTY-NINE

THIS WAS UNACCEPTABLE. Morpheus had once again caused his lover and his familiar pain—and yet, his actions had followed the only conceivable course open to him. What could he have done differently, given everything that was at stake?

Somehow, with Hugh clutching at his lapels as though he wished to rend the fabric with the force of his grip, the imminent breakdown of human society seemed to hold less weight than it had when Morpheus had driven a kitchen knife through his own ribs.

"Fuckin'... *bastard,*" Hugh said wetly, the words fluttering against the side of Morpheus' throat.

Iridaceae had scooped up the cat and was holding the little beast tight to her chest, as though for comfort. Both of them looked ill-tempered and bedraggled in the spitting rain.

"Perhaps we should return to the cottage," Morpheus said softly, not releasing Hugh from his supportive embrace.

The human raised his head, craning it to look down at the corpse. "But... what about... we can't just—"

He cut himself off sharply, and Morpheus got the impression he couldn't quite bring himself to say, *we can't just leave your body here.*

The abandoned construct of flesh and blood was a strange and pitiful thing, lying like a discarded marionette with the rain washing its congealed blood into the forest loam.

"Allow me," Morpheus said, stretching out a hand and recalling the inert building blocks of mortal life. It was almost shocking, how little of himself the physical form comprised. It had felt all-encompassing—indeed, quite overwhelming at times—during the span of days when he'd been irrevocably trapped inside it.

"... *oh*," Hugh breathed, watching the trail of sparkling matter swirl up to Morpheus' fingers and disappear inside him.

The boning knife teetered and fell to the ground as the body that had been holding it upright dissolved. Not a speck of blood clung to the steel blade. Iridaceae crouched down and picked it up with a sour expression, supporting Baphometh in her other arm.

"Now we may depart," Morpheus said with finality, turning away from the scattered, empty clothing… all that remained of his mortal existence.

He had a feeling that, were he to ask Iridaceae, she would confirm that Hugh had leapt directly from reawakening after death into searching the woods for him, with no time in between for his own recovery.

Morpheus retraced the overgrown path leading from the cottage to the clearing, treading slowly and supporting Hugh with an arm around his back. Brambles that would have torn at his clothing and skin when he was mortal slid past without catching. The walk was not a long one, and soon they were approaching the open front door of Hugh's little house.

Morpheus frowned at the cracks in the plaster ceiling and walls as they entered — a reminder of the explosion that had precipitated his actions. More repairs that the human would have to perform if he wished to continue a pantomime of normalcy. He shut the front door — so recently replaced after Phobetor's intrusion.

Your reach exceeds your grasp, Phobetor, Thanatus had told the God of Fear. *Have a care, before someone loses patience and slices your arm off.*

Morpheus knew he was ill-suited to wage war against another god, but his brother had to be stopped. The knowledge that his uncle would not intervene on humanity's behalf — that his *parents* would not intervene — made him heartsore.

Someone had to be the one to say *enough.* If there was no one, else, then it fell to him. But also, there was Hugh.

When it came to his human lover, what Morpheus had been doing before was no longer good enough. He led Hugh through to the kitchen and settled him in a chair, his chest aching at the man's uncharacteristic pliancy. Morpheus had brought Hugh to this sorry state, and he had done it while trying to protect the human from the consequences of his association with a god.

It was time to rethink the mental paradigm he had assembled piecemeal, like an ill-designed quilt.

Hugh would have stormed Thanatus' gates to act as Morpheus' messenger when Iridaceae could not, had such a thing not been precluded by the terms of the very wager that made him immortal in the first place. Hugh hadn't shied away from fighting Morpheus' battles, whether alone or at his lover's side.

Morpheus had made the mistake of thinking he could dissuade the human from doing so, rather than accepting him as an ally… as a true partner.

The problem was, such alliances between denizens of the Night Lands and the Sublunary had been vanishingly rare over the millennia — and when they did happen, they often ended in tragedy. But Hugh had earned the right to make such decisions for himself, and Morpheus had been wrong to try and wrest that agency from him.

He lowered himself into a crouch, eyeing the human critically.

"You are not yet recovered from your attempt to intercede on my behalf," he said. "You must drink water and eat something substantial. Then, before you rest, we must talk."

Hugh gazed up at him blearily — the picture of a man who'd swilled an entire bottle of vodka, been suffocated to death, then woken up and gone trudging through a damp forest in the rain.

"Not hungry," he croaked.

Morpheus snorted. "I am not so ignorant of humanity that I am unaware of the cure for a hangover."

"There's leftover shepherd's pie in the refrigerator," Iridaceae said, letting Baphometh leap down from her arms. She tossed the knife into the sink with a clatter. "I'll heat some up for him in the microwave."

She still sounded furious. Morpheus couldn't blame her.

"Thank you," he told her, retrieving a glass of cool water while she worked and placing it firmly in front of Hugh on the kitchen table. When Hugh grudgingly lifted it to his lips, Morpheus gave an approving nod. Satisfied, he went to get paracetamol from the bathroom and a blanket from the bedroom.

Upon his return, he placed the former on the table next to the half-drunk glass and draped the latter over Hugh's shoulders. The microwave dinged, and Morpheus set the reheated shepherd's pie in front of the human as well. Hugh glared at the plate balefully, but he took the fork Morpheus handed him and began picking at the food.

Within moments, his body's needs took over, and he was shoveling it into his face like a starving man—or at least, like a man who'd had to rebuild a fair amount of fatally damaged tissue in a very short stretch of time. Morpheus took a seat across from him and waited until he slowed down a bit before speaking.

"We must discuss our next steps," he began.

Hugh looked at him warily, doubtless expecting another exhortation to stay well out of things.

"What do you mean, 'our next steps'?" he asked. "You've got your powers back, don't you?"

"I do." Morpheus turned his attention to Iridaceae. "It is important that someone go to the Night Lands to check on my realm. Iridaceae, I wish you to travel ahead and deliver a message to the oneiri. Tell them that my return is imminent."

"You don't want to go yourself?" Iridaceae asked, sounding both surprised and skeptical.

"Hugh and I will be along shortly," he said, drawing a sharp glance from the human in question. "If the oneiri are aware of my impending arrival, they will have time to return to any duties they may have been shirking in my absence. Which, in turn, will save me having to punish them."

Iridaceae made a considering noise and shrugged. "All right, then. Do you want me to use the opal?"

"Yes." He beckoned her to his side and touched the milky stone hanging at her throat with one finger. He filled it with as much of his power as would fit, musing that he would need to get her a larger one at some point in the near future.

When she started to straighten away, he caught her slender hand, stopping her. "You are a loyal and steadfast friend, Iridaceae. I regret the pain my actions have caused you. If anything is badly amiss in our home, come straight back here to safety. Otherwise, Hugh and I will see you within an hour or two."

Iridaceae looked taken aback, as well she might. "You didn't cause me pain," she said. "You caused me anger, because you're a *bloody infuriating prat.*"

"I fear I have no defense against the accusation," he told her.

"Hmph!" she said. Her amber-gold eyes fell on Hugh. "I suppose I'll see you in a little bit, then."

"And how is *that* supposed to work?" Hugh asked plaintively.

But Iridaceae only shrugged before transforming into an owl. She flapped her wings twice and slipped through the veil, disappearing from the mortal realm.

Hugh's bewildered gaze returned to Morpheus, who inclined his head in acknowledgement of the human's understandable confusion.

"I am not a good choice of combatant to battle my brother for control in the Sublunary," he said. "However, it appears there is no one else willing to stand against him. So—as you have made it very clear that you will not allow me to fight this war without you—I humbly request that you accompany me to the Night Lands as my partner and ally."

Hugh just stared at him.

"You're having me on," he said eventually.

"I am not," Morpheus told him. "It is likely that the war for humanity's soul will take place in the mortal realm. However, there is information I need to extract from my uncle, first... or, failing that, from some other source within the realm of the gods."

For the first time since Morpheus' reappearance in the clearing, the faintest hint of wry humor colored Hugh's tone. "Wait. Are you seriously saying you want to put me in the same room as Thanatus, after the infamous fifteenth century testicle-kicking incident?"

Morpheus raised an eyebrow. "Were you not attempting to reach Thanatus yourself, mere hours ago?"

"Well, *yes*," Hugh said, looking at him as though he was mentally deficient. "I was... *back when we had the leverage of the favor he owed you.*

Which, I gather, we don't anymore." He shook his head sharply, then winced, presumably when the sudden motion pained him. "Okay, fine. So, you want me to go visit the Grim Reaper with you. But how does that even *work*—I mean, from a purely practical perspective? Does this mean you're going to rip out my soul again, like your brother did when he kidnapped me?"

Morpheus held Hugh's gaze, unblinking. "Not at all. I am the God of Dreams, my hunter. You have visited my realm many times, even though we haven't previously ventured much outside the walls of your own subconscious. To join me in the Night Lands, you need only do the one thing your body requires most right now. You must *sleep*."

THIRTY

IT WAS ABSOLUTELY typical that the moment someone said, '*You need to sleep now,*' Hugh's brain decided to do its impression of a caffeinated hamster running in a wheel. He'd been *dead*, for fuck's sake. Then he'd woken up and had his heart ripped out when he'd found his lover's body, only to have it clumsily stitched back together a few minutes later when Morpheus reappeared unharmed.

Now Morpheus wanted him as an ally. As a proper partner. A part of Hugh was still waiting for the punchline... for someone to pop out with a video camera and tell him it had all been a prank.

The larger part thought Morpheus might actually mean it. Which led to the very natural question of what he, as a human, would be expected to do as part of a war between the gods. At the moment, he wouldn't have bet money on his ability to tie his own shoelaces—so, that part of things was more than a little worrying.

You've fought in wars before, he told himself firmly. The problem was, he'd hated every goddamned minute of every war he'd ever been stuck in, across his entire eight hundred bloody years of living.

"You are ruminating," Morpheus observed, frowning at him.

"You think?" Hugh asked, wishing ardently that he wasn't already battling the hangover from hell—because a drink or ten would have been quite helpful right about now.

"I have exceeded your psychological capacity for stress," Morpheus said, his frown deepening.

"Oh my god, *fuck you*," Hugh told him.

Morpheus hesitated for a moment. "I'm sure I deserve that."

"*Yes, you fucking do!*" Hugh shouted. Then he winced as his head rang with pain in response to the increased volume. "You fucking *do*," he repeated, this time in a whisper.

"Come." Morpheus urged him up from the kitchen table. "I have found over the past months that bathing can be quite restorative after facing adversity."

Hugh wavered over the prospect of shouting some more. After a moment's hesitation, he gave up on the idea… mostly based on how much it would make his head pound.

"Fine." He allowed himself to be guided—because anything else felt like far too much work. There was also the small matter that he still smelled like a corpse, and he could, in fact, use a wash.

At least the food and drink had settled his stomach a bit. Maybe the painkillers would kick in soon and mute the pounding inside his skull. *That* would be a gift from the fucking gods, right there.

Rather than taking him to the bathroom where he'd so recently knocked on death's door and been summarily turned away, Morpheus led him to the boot room where Hugh had installed a shower to sluice off the dirt when he came home filthy and mud-encrusted from shoeing horses.

The damage here seemed to be less than in the main part of the cottage—but rather than being a relief, that observation only reminded Hugh about the bomb in the church.

"I should check the news," he said. "Find out what happened to the village. They may need help. Volunteers."

Morpheus paused for the space of a heartbeat before speaking. "I understand why you would wish to seek information, and your willingness to help does you credit."

Hugh followed the thought to its inevitable conclusion. "But it's more important to go after Phobetor and try to cut off the insanity at its root." He scrubbed at his face. "No, you're right. Besides, I can barely walk in a straight line at the moment."

Morpheus' tense posture relaxed minutely. "Sleep would still be the wisest course for your recovery, whether you accompany me on my errand in the Night Lands or not."

"Your point is taken." Hugh reached into the shower and turned on the taps, adjusting them hotter than he normally would have. He removed his clothing as the water warmed up, feeling every single one of his centuries in the pull and creak of his aching muscles.

He didn't expect a newly minted godling to slip into the utilitarian shower with him as he stepped under the spray. Morpheus' elegant clothing dissipated into the ether as the cool, lithe form joined him. Marble-pale arms wrapped around him from behind, and Hugh—weak willed fool that he was— slumped into that sure embrace.

The manic brain-hamster slowed in its wheel as deft hands reached for the soap, lathering it over every inch of his body with sure movements. Shampoo was next, and Hugh couldn't quite stifle a broken whimper as fingers scrubbed circles on his scalp. His headache eased beneath the delicious tingles, or possibly that was the paracetamol finally kicking in.

Conditioner followed a thorough rinse... because Morpheus had turned out to be a vain creature as a human. Not, he reflected, that conditioner had ever done much to tame the wild dandelion fluff of his companion's hair.

"Think I can sleep now," Hugh slurred, the tension flowing out of his muscles and down the drain with the soapy water.

"Good," Morpheus murmured, running soft hands over his body in a way that threatened to wake parts of him besides his brain. "Though, if you are feeling somewhat recovered physically, then perhaps I can do something more to ensure your rest."

Fingers cupped Hugh's cock, assessing its heft. Hugh made a wordless, vaguely affirmative noise, followed by a groan of disappointment when the fingers retreated. Morpheus turned off the water and chivvied Hugh out of the shower, rubbing him down with the towel hanging nearby.

When Hugh turned, thinking to return the favor, it was to find that Morpheus was already as dry as though he'd never stepped into the shower in the first place. *Perks of being a god,* Hugh thought, allowing himself to be herded naked down the hallway to the bedroom. Here, the ceiling hadn't fared as well. Small chunks of plaster had rained down on the bed.

Morpheus scowled and left Hugh leaning on the dresser while he swept the sheets and blankets from the mattress, replacing them with fresh linens from the closet. Once he was satisfied, he guided Hugh onto the bed and slid in behind him.

Hugh was still distantly convinced that he needed to hold onto his grudge over Morpheus' reckless behavior for at least several more days, but it was difficult when smooth flesh spooned him from behind, and an artist's fingers trailed over his chest and stomach.

"Iridaceae isn't the only one who's still angry at you." The protest was a weak one.

"I know," Morpheus said quietly, his hand closing around Hugh's half-hard cock.

Hugh made a choked noise and closed his eyes, giving himself permission to have this moment after believing he might never have such a thing again. Morpheus worked him with casual mastery and a lover's familiarity, his own cock probing between Hugh's arse cheeks to slide back and forth through the sensitive valley there. His lover flexed his hips, and with each stroke, his hard tip nudged Hugh's sac from behind.

Smooth lips pressed kisses to Hugh's shoulder, then upward to brush the tendon running along the side of his neck. The hand around his prick guided him effortlessly to a blissful plateau that promised an eventual shattering orgasm on the other side.

Unfortunately, sleep claimed him before his climax did.

When he opened his eyes, he was in a familiar palace—if an unfamiliar part of it. Still, he recognized this elegant grandeur... this cool color scheme of blue and gold and green. A medieval peasant's vision of the lord's manor.

He was as naked as he'd been in his bed at home. Morpheus, who was very much fully dressed, continued to work his cock, holding him on the edge of ecstasy. Only now, Hugh's throbbing headache was gone, and he was reclining on a decadent chaise longue with Morpheus perched on the edge next to his hips.

But... they were not alone in the room. A dozen other people wandered through the well-appointed space, chatting with each other casually while occasionally tossing glances their way. Hugh's jolt of humiliated panic lasted only long enough for him to realize that all of the casual onlookers... were *also* Morpheus.

"What the—?" he asked blankly.

The Morpheus who was seated next to him quirked an eyebrow. "As we have discussed on multiple previous occasion, it's *your* dream, my hunter." His lips pursed thoughtfully. "Though perhaps it is one better explored in more depth some other time."

Hugh gaped at him. "Uh..."

One of the other versions of Morpheus approached. "Good evening," the newcomer said, reaching down to swipe a thumb over Hugh's lower lip with casual possession. "I see you did not exaggerate. He really is quite appealing."

"I did say so," the first Morpheus replied mildly, adding a clever twist to his steady stroke that had Hugh seeing stars. "Perhaps at our next meeting, I will strap him to a piece of furniture and place him out for our public use."

"What an excellent idea." The thumb teasing his lower lip pushed past the barrier of Hugh's teeth, pressing heavily against his tongue. The hand on his cock gave another twisting stroke, and he came with a startled yelp, his entire body convulsing beneath the shock of it. His vision whited out, the pleasure stretching impossibly long and deep.

When he once again became aware of his surroundings, he was curled on the chaise with Morpheus, secure in his lover's embrace. They were alone, and they were both clothed.

"Did you mean what you said?" Hugh asked hoarsely.

"Which part?" Morpheus replied.

Hugh hesitated, picturing the room full of Morpheuses watching him come all over himself. "Never mind," he mumbled.

Morpheus made an agreeable noise. "As you wish. When you have quite recovered, we should leave in search of those answers I need."

Hugh tried to get his bearings. "Okay. But... just to be clear, I'm still dreaming, right?"

"In a manner of speaking. Your body is safely asleep in your bed. However, in the normal course of things, you would have passed out of REM sleep by now. I am holding you here so that you may accompany me outside the usual bounds of your unconscious mind. So, I suppose you could say this is no longer your dream, since I have taken control of it."

"If you say so." Hugh cautiously rolled into a sitting position. The heady flush of orgasm still pumped through his veins, but he felt none of the usual languor that should have accompanied it. If anything, he felt energized—no longer at the mercy of his frail human body after the latest round of abuse it had undergone in the real world. "Let's go, then. Time to see if the Grim Reaper would benefit from another kick in the balls after all."

THIRTY-ONE

THE GRIM REAPER, as it turned out, would *not* be receiving another kick in the balls, since he was nowhere to be found within the realm of Tartarus.

Tartarus.

Hugh was in fucking *Tartarus*… or at least, his sleeping mind was here.

"So, this is where I would have ended up if I'd died like a normal person?" he asked, gazing around at the desolate, stony landscape.

"You would have passed through it, certainly," Morpheus said. "Whether or not you would have stayed is a rather thorny philosophical question. Many souls — most, I daresay — seek the infinite sleep of nonexistence."

Hugh swallowed hard, unable to even imagine such a thing.

"Others linger in the more pleasant areas of my uncle's realm," Morpheus continued, gesturing to the disconcerting shadows darting around them in Hugh's peripheral vision. "Some become shades. Some are unable to escape the draw of the pit; too weighed down by their own guilt when confronted with ultimate knowledge of their crimes."

His voice had gone all detached and monotoney during that last part. Hugh wanted to ask him more about that… but he also very much did *not* want to ask, for fear of what answer he might receive.

"Would I be happier not knowing what's making that bellowing noise?" he asked instead.

The terrible, muffled cries were so deep and powerful that Hugh could feel them vibrating through the stone around him.

"It is safe to say that you would be happier, yes," Morpheus said. "Unfortunately, in the absence of my uncle, it is they we will be meeting with. That noise is coming from the Titans. The pit of Tartarus has been their eternal prison, ever since the last great war."

Hugh stopped cold for a moment, only to hurry forward again when the shades lurking in his periphery circled closer to him. Morpheus turned to face him; elegant brows furrowed.

"You need not accompany me if you do not wish to," he said. "I can return you safely to your bed in the Sublunary and proceed alone."

Hugh's mouth opened. There were words that should be coming out, but somehow, they'd all piled up in his throat, unable to escape.

Are you crazy?

What the hell are you thinking?

You just got back from being dead, why are you in such a hurry to chat with a bunch of monsters trapped in a pit?

He swallowed, feeling his throat click even though this was a dream.

"I'm not going anywhere, you prat," he said. "So, on a scale of one to ten, exactly how dangerous is this likely to be?"

"It will be dangerous," Morpheus said. "Though perhaps not in the way you are thinking."

"I have no idea what that means," Hugh replied tiredly. "Before we go, what are we trying to find out? You said you needed information. Why do you think these monsters have it? They don't exactly sound like the friendly sort."

As though in response to his words, the roars grew into tortured wails.

"When I asked Thanatus what had happened to our family to make us fight so, he implied that there was some sort of inciting incident," Morpheus said, his expression growing thoughtful. "*'Nothing that can be repaired,'* he told me. I wish to know the details of what happened to us, despite my uncle's apparent reticence on the subject."

Hugh let that sink in for a moment. "You mean, it wasn't always like this? You all used to get along?"

"That might be overstating things. Certainly, some of us were closer than others." Morpheus gazed into nothingness—his expression strangely intent. "Phobetor has always been abrasive. That is doubtless related to his function. But Fear and Nightmare overlap. I never had the sense that he harbored ill will toward me, back when we were younger."

If that was the case, then something really *had* changed. Phobetor's current vendetta against Morpheus gave every impression of being personal.

"Phantasos and I were once close," Morpheus went on. "Even now, I find myself shocked by his betrayal, and his defection to Phobetor's side. Fear and Fantasy are not completely unrelated, it is true. However, they do make rather strange bedfellows."

In truth, Hugh was still struggling with the theoretical separation between Morpheus and his brothers' *functions*, and their *personhood*. Morpheus himself was very much an individual, with his own traits and foibles. But he was also the God of Dreams, and Hugh wasn't vain enough to believe he had the first idea what that actually entailed.

He'd seen the effects of its absence, it was true — when Morpheus had been trapped in a bunker for eighty years, and the mortal creatures of Earth had suffered for it. But he still couldn't seem to map that understanding onto the proud, soft-spoken creature who'd massaged shampoo into his hair and tucked him into bed with tender caresses to send him off to sleep.

"I don't think I understand any of this," he admitted with a sigh. "Come on, then. Let's go interrogate some horrific creatures from the dawn of time."

"Yes." Morpheus sounded grim. "If you will permit me, my hunter — it would be best if you do not attract the attention of those we seek to visit."

He opened his arm as though to invite Hugh into an embrace. Hugh — with no clue exactly what was being asked of him — stepped into it. Rather than being pressed against Morpheus' familiar form, Hugh found himself pulled *inside* his lover. His sense of physicality did not change, as such... but now he saw their surroundings through Morpheus' eyes and felt them through Morpheus' skin.

His mind accepted this impossibility in the same way it accepted other manifestations of dream-logic. It didn't feel alarming at all. In fact, it felt quite natural. When Morpheus stepped sideways through reality, reappearing in impenetrable darkness, Hugh knew he should have been afraid. But perhaps

Morpheus' glacial calm had also enveloped him, because he only felt curious.

Curious… and *protected.*

The tortured wails of vast beings too large for Hugh to comprehend rent the air. Morpheus did not flinch, instead stepping forward and lifting a hand, palm up in offering. A flame flickered in his cupped palm, growing larger until it cast a circle of warm light within the endless darkness.

The light fell on five massive figures arrayed around them, illuminating them piecemeal. Hugh got a confused impression of too many arms and too few eyes… on a scale he couldn't hope to comprehend.

"Your Magnificences," Morpheus called out, his voice clear and strong. "I humbly beg an audience."

One of the creatures bent down as though to see him more clearly, the light glinting off its single huge eye. "Little godling," it rumbled in a voice like boulders tumbling together. "You dare return to us so soon after your fall?"

"I do," Morpheus replied, unruffled.

Hugh wondered, with a flutter of uncertainty, if his sense that these beings could snuff out the God of Dreams like a guttering candle flame was accurate.

"Why should we talk to you, when we could consume you instead?" rumbled a different voice. Dozens of chitinous arms rustled together, as though in anticipation of slicing and cutting.

"I bring you light," Morpheus said, setting the flame down on the pitch-black floor in front of him—the movement graceful as a courtier's bow. "Light to burn for a hundred years, given freely and with no expectation of return."

The mountainous figures loomed closer, as though drawn to the flicker of supernatural flame. Hugh wondered, with an unexpected pang, how long it had been since they'd had either light or warmth in this terrible place.

"We need no light!" roared another of the Cyclopes. "The souls of the damned sustain us!"

Morpheus wisely did not point out that all five of the Titans were straining toward the flame like moths toward a lit torch. He bowed again. "That is most certainly true, Your Magnificences. Yet it is my gift to you, all the same."

The Hundred-Hander chittered. "A gift, with no expectation of return?" it asked. "What nonsense! Tell us why you have come here, little godling."

Morpheus bowed even lower, until his forehead nearly touched the void serving inexplicably as the floor beneath them.

"You are correct, of course. Should you wish to honor me with a gift in turn, I would ask for information. You are the oldest and most venerable creatures within the Night Lands."

One of the Cyclopes tilted its head, in an almost doglike movement. "Information? What sort of information is worth the possibility of destruction at our hands?"

"I must know what has befallen the grandchildren of Kronos and Chaos," Morpheus said, straightening from his obeisance. "The Sublunary is in danger. Unless the balance of power between the gods is restored, I fear a new war may spill into the Night Lands as well."

The bound Titans stared down at the tiny god in their midst for a long moment. And then, they began to laugh, the sound shaking the walls of the pit until it seemed the entire structure might crumble to dust around them.

THIRTY-TWO

MORPHEUS STEADIED himself against the convulsion of reality caused by the Titans' deafening laughter. The Pit of Tartarus had been created solely to contain the monstrous Old Gods. It would not fail beneath something so simple as their merriment.

However, that did not mean it was wise to trifle with such creatures. Coming here at all had been a risk. That risk had not diminished with the Titans' apparent amusement.

Yet, he could not back down. He needed answers, and he was unwilling to wait for them one moment longer.

"Is a second war between the gods truly cause for such laughter?" he called, pitching his voice to cut through the uproarious noise. From within, he could feel Hugh's trepidation as though it was a part of him—indeed it *was* a part of him, with the human's awareness tucked away inside himself.

Gradually, the laughter died away. One of the Cyclopes leaned down again, its single eye looming in the light from the flame.

"No, no, little creature," it said. "Such a war will cause widespread destruction and strife across the realms. We are not laughing at the prospect of an imminent battle. We are laughing at *you*."

Morpheus hesitated, seeking the best approach to extract more information from them. "I see. Will you deign to enlighten me on the details of the joke?"

"*Enlighten*," one of the Hundred-Handers echoed. "Ha! Yes, I suppose there is symmetry to that. Has he not *enlightened* us with his little gift of fire?"

"Hmm," said the Cyclopes. "Yes, that is pleasing wordplay. Very well, little godling. You ask us what has befallen the grandchildren of Kronos and Chaos."

"That is correct," Morpheus confirmed.

"And yet, you are asking the wrong question."

He frowned. "Then... what is the *right* question?"

A low, rumbling chuckle rolled through the darkness.

"Perhaps you should cease wondering what has happened to your brothers..." The Cyclopes tilted its head, examining him closely. "... and instead, ask yourself what has happened to your *sister*."

A dark pit opened behind Morpheus' ribcage, though he could not have explained why. The creature's words made no *sense*.

"I have no sister," he said blankly.

He thought he detected pity behind the Titan's unfathomably huge eye — the kind of pity one might bestow on someone too dim to understand the answer to a simple question.

"Exactly," it replied.

Morpheus stood frozen, once again feeling as though the icy darkness of the pit was spreading through him, driving out his sense of self and replacing it with raw voidstuff.

"*Morpheus.*" Hugh's familiar presence pricked at the edge of his shrinking awareness. "*We need to leave now.*"

But he continued to stand paralyzed in the center of the looming circle of Titans, unable to tear his eyes away from the pitiful flicker of flame illuminating them in ever-shifting chiaroscuro.

"*Leof!*" Hugh's voice came sharper, his shadowy interior presence spiking with fear. "*Go now! Get us out of here!*"

Without thought, Morpheus wrenched them sideways, out of the void and away from the monsters trapped within. They reappeared on a desolate plain; Hugh's unconscious mind once again standing separate and steadfast beside him.

Heavy clouds roiled overhead. Wind whipped the scraggly skeletons of trees.

Hugh staggered beneath the onslaught, catching himself before he could fall to the stony ground.

"*I have no sister,*" Morpheus said again, as though repeating it might somehow banish the cold emptiness that had opened within him.

Warm hands grasped his shoulders.

"Yeah, you already said." Hugh ducked his head, forcing Morpheus to meet his eyes. "So why do you look like someone just ripped out your heart and stomped on it?"

Morpheus stared at him as though that warm brown gaze could act as a lifeline back to logic and sanity. "I... I don't..." He shook his head sharply. "This makes no *sense.*"

Hugh looked as out of his depth as any human might under the circumstances, but he didn't release his grip as his brow furrowed in concentration. "That *thing* said something happened to her. So... did you have a sister before?"

Abruptly, Morpheus recognized the hole in his chest for what it was—a negative impression left by something important that had been lost. The absence of something vital and dear. Anger coalesced, bitter and choking in his throat. It coated his words like acid when he spoke, the atmosphere around them wavering beneath the power of his burgeoning rage.

"I must speak to Thanatus. *Now.*"

His uncle had not returned to the secluded castle clinging to the cliffs of Perdition. Morpheus turned to the nearest shade and hissed, "Bring your master to me this instant, or I will *unmake you.*"

When the shadow didn't move fast enough, Morpheus let the power that had been crackling around him like barely leashed electricity explode outward. The nearest wall twisted, the stone transforming into a thousand gray doves that flew away into the Night Lands in a deafening flurry of wings. Timbers creaked in the ceiling above them, suddenly without support.

The shade fled with a terrified shriek, leaving him alone with Hugh and a myriad of swirling questions.

Hugh grasped his bicep. The contact was grounding, for all that Morpheus still felt as though he might go the same way as the wall, his body and mind flying apart in countless different directions.

"Do you think Thanatus knows about this? About a sister you can't remember?" Hugh asked.

'*Nothing that can be repaired,*' the God of Death had told him, when Morpheus asked what had happened to their fractured family.

"I don't know," he said hoarsely.

Scarcely had the words fallen to silence when black vapor swirled through a gap in the veil, before coalescing into Thanatus' imposing form. He took one look at the missing wall and the trickle of stone dust sifting down from the unsupported ceiling, then he turned on Morpheus and Hugh with a thunderous expression.

Morpheus had no idea what his own face must look like. He lunged forward, fingers grasping claw-like at his uncle's robes, and shoved the God of Death backward until his broad shoulders impacted the nearest pillar. He had no illusions — only the element of surprise had allowed him this small moment of physical domination over the older and more powerful god.

Before Thanatus could blast him backward in a fit of rage, Morpheus snarled five heavy words into the air between them.

"*Tell me about my sister.*"

258

THIRTY-THREE

HUGH HAD THE distinct impression that he was about two seconds away from witnessing an all-out battle between deities. Thanatus had raised a hand, swirls of black nothingness streaming from it, while around them, the remaining walls of the castle wavered as though they, too, might suddenly transform into birds and fly away.

Gritting his teeth, Hugh barged forward, grabbing Morpheus' shoulder with one hand, and Thanatus' shoulder with the other. He stood about as much chance of physically wrenching the pair apart as a snowball stood in the Mojave Desert, but nevertheless, he shouted, "*Stop!*" at the top of his lungs.

Thanatus stared down at him with obsidian eyes, as though a cockroach had just stood up on its hind legs and started reciting the Magna Carta.

"We visited the monsters in the pit," Hugh said, before any wholesale smiting could occur. "The Titans, I mean. They told Morpheus that his sister was gone."

Happily, the smiting remained on hold for the moment.

"You returned to the pit?" Thanatus demanded in disbelief, the words directed toward Morpheus.

Hugh answered for him, since Morpheus still looked like someone contemplating the rampant disassembly of local reality. "Yeah. We did. So maybe we could all stop trying to kill each other for a minute, and you could tell us what the fuck is going on, instead? This is your *niece* we're talking about, if what the monsters said was true. It's his *sister*. He deserves to know what happened!"

Very slowly, Thanatus lowered his raised hand. The threatening tendrils of impenetrable voidstuff thinned, and finally dissipated altogether.

Morpheus did not relinquish his claw like grip on the God of Death's robes, but the walls of the castle stopped wavering, at least.

"*Speak*, Uncle," he spat.

Thanatus slapped Morpheus' hand away, the power behind the gesture sending the younger god stumbling back a step. Then the dark figure of Death whirled away, his black robes billowing, and paced a few steps across the room. He came to a stop in front of the no longer extant wall, not looking at either of them.

"She was lost," he said, after an extended pause. "Through her own foolishness. And in her absence, the balance of the cosmos lies in disarray."

Morpheus stared at him. He looked hollowed out—as though the discovery of his unmourned loss had physically diminished him, somehow.

"Why do I not remember her?" he asked, his tone faint.

Thanatus made a sharp, frustrated gesture with one hand. "It is a function of the way in which her existence was destroyed."

"What do you mean?" Morpheus demanded.

Thanatus turned on him, his fathomless black eyes burning. "She fled to the Sublunary to take a human lover, leaving her godhood hidden in a clay jar so she could live as a mortal."

Hugh winced, even if Morpheus didn't. That story hit far too close to home. No wonder Thanatus had exploded when he found out what Morpheus had done with the opal pendant. He must have feared a repeat performance of what had befallen his lost niece.

"What does that have to do with Morpheus not remembering her, though?" Hugh asked, aware that he was treading dangerously by continuing to court the God of Death's attention. "Phobetor and Phantasos didn't suddenly forget that Morpheus existed, just because he shunted his powers into that necklace."

Thanatus' lips curled back. The expression wasn't a smile. "Someone released the contents of the jar. Her divinity was scattered to the four winds, and when her mortal body eventually perished of old age, nothing at all of her remained."

"I should still remember," Morpheus whispered.

"Remember *what*?" Thanatus asked. "Elpis is gone. Her godhood is gone. There is nothing to remember."

Hugh couldn't help noticing the chink in that argument. "I dunno, mate. *You* seem to be doing a good enough job of it."

The full weight of Thanatus' gaze fell on him. "On the contrary. I have no memory whatsoever of the goddess known as Elpis."

Hugh scowled. "Funny. Because it sure sounds like you do."

"Knowledge of Elpis resides in only one place," Thanatus growled. "As you and my meddlesome nephew have just discovered."

"The Titans," Morpheus breathed. "You gleaned this knowledge the same way we did. From them."

"Yes," Thanatus agreed. "They existed before the current reality came into being. They are not constrained by the same laws as the rest of us."

"Well, you were clearly more successful at pumping them for information than we were," Hugh said, his patience nearly exhausted. "So, tell us why her disappearance screwed things up so badly in the mortal realm. What was she the goddess of, anyway?"

"Hope," said the God of Death. "Elpis was the embodiment of Hope."

—◆—

When it became obvious that Thanatus had no more insight to offer on the subject, Hugh urged Morpheus to return them to his own lands. He seemed dazed; overwhelmed by what he'd just learned… not that Hugh found this surprising.

But before he could start properly questioning Morpheus about the implications of Hope having been lost in the Sublunary, his surroundings shifted again. He awoke to find himself curled naked in his bedroom in the cottage, just as he had been when he'd fallen asleep. A familiar lean form pressed up against his back, trembling.

Hugh squirmed beneath the covers, twisting until he could get his arms around Morpheus and pull his lover into a tight embrace.

"Hey. *Hey*," he rasped. "I've got you. C'mon, Morpheus — this is a *good* thing. It's the first real clue we've found to explain what's gone wrong in the world. Maybe we can use this somehow to counter Phobetor. To *fix* things."

Morpheus shook his head, his slender body a single block of tension. "No… don't you *see*, Hugh?" he murmured into Hugh's collarbone. "*Hopes* and *dreams*."

Hugh continued to hold him. "Sorry, *leof*. Tiny human brain over here. I'm afraid I really *don't* see. Are you saying that your sister's absence allowed Phobetor to become more powerful? Because hope still exists, you know. Even if it doesn't have its own goddess anymore."

Morpheus pushed away from his embrace and sat up. His beautiful features looked haunted in the morning light — gray skinned and gaunt. "You don't understand. *Think*, Hugh. Living creatures still dreamed during the eighty years I was bound. But only after a fashion."

Hugh caught his breath, rolling into a sitting position as well. "Oh."

They had still dreamed, it was true. But only in a stunted and tortuous manner that was more torment than respite. Had the same thing happened to hope, somehow? Was what Hugh now knew as 'hope' only the twisted and half-forgotten remains of something better? Of what it was truly meant to be?

"It's even worse than that, though," Morpheus went on. "If the Titans are the only ones who remember her, she must have disappeared a very long time ago. Millennia, at the least. The mortal realm may have grown slowly more unbalanced as the centuries passed—"

"But it's only in the past few decades that things really started sliding off the rails," Hugh finished. A terrible realization dawned, stilling the breath in his lungs.

Morpheus nodded, as though he could see through Hugh's skull to read his sudden understanding.

"Precisely," he said, his voice a brittle monotone. "It was my own capture in nineteen forty that precipitated the final decline of the Sublunary. In the absence of both my gift and my sister's, the world reached a tipping point."

Hugh swallowed the dry lump that had formed in his throat. "Okay, but... can it be tipped back somehow? Now that we understand more about what happened?"

"I don't know."

He'd never heard the God of Dreams sound so lost before.

Determination stiffened Hugh's spine. "Then it sounds like we've got work to do. Starting with figuring out exactly what your sister did with her powers, and if there's any way to undo it."

"Thanatus has already said there is not."

"He also said he doesn't remember any of this for himself," Hugh pointed out. "So, I'm not sure what he could be using as a basis for that conclusion. Besides, do we really have another choice?"

Silence fell.

"Perhaps not," Morpheus allowed, after a lengthy pause. "It will not be easy, Hugh. If Phobetor discovers this information as well, he will seek to oppose us."

"Then we'll stand against him," Hugh said. "Together. We were going to do that anyway, weren't we?"

Morpheus held Hugh's gaze for long moments, his crystalline blue eyes unfathomably deep.

"I suppose we were, my hunter," he said at last. "Very well, then. We will face him together… in *hope* for a better future."

finis

Morpheus and Hugh's adventure concludes in
Book Three: *Eventide*.

To discover more books by this author, visit
www.rasteffan.com